Sophie Loves Jimmy

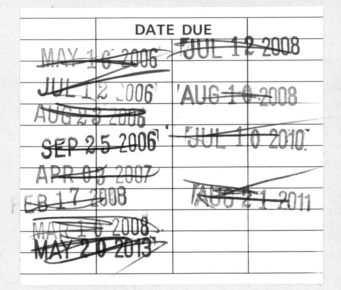

Other books in the growing Faithgirlz!™ library

The Faithgirlz!™ Bible
NIV Faithgirlz!™ Backpack Bible
My Faithgirlz!™ Journal

The Sophie Series

Sophie's World (Book One)
Sophie's Secret (Book Two)
Sophie and the Scoundrels (Book Three)
Sophie's Irish Showdown (Book Four)
Sophie's First Dance? (Book Five)
Sophie's Stormy Summer (Book Six)
Sophie Breaks the Code (Book Seven)
Sophie Tracks a Thief (Book Eight)
Sophie Flakes Out (Book Nine)
Sophie Loses the Lead (Book Eleven)
Sophie's Encore (Book Twelve)

Blog On Series

Grace Notes (Book One)
Love, Annie (Book Two)
Just Jazz (Book Three)
Storm Rising (Book Four)

Nonfiction

No Boys Allowed: Devotions for Girls
Girlz Rock: Devotions for You
Chick Chat: More Devotions for Girls
Shine On, Girl!: Devotions to Keep You Sparkling

Check out www.faithgirlz.com

faiThGirLz!™

Sophie Loves Jimmy

Nancy Rue

zonder**kidz**

ZONDERVAN.COM/
AUTHOR**TRACKER**

zonder**kidz**
The children's group of Zondervan

www.zonderkidz.com

Requests for information should be addressed to:
Zonderkidz, 5300 Patterson Ave. SE
Grand Rapids, Michigan 49530

Library of Congress Cataloging-in-Publication Data

Rue, Nancy N.
    Sophie loves Jimmy / Nancy Rue.
      p. cm. – (The Sophie series ; bk. 10) (Faithgirlz!)
    Summary: Paired with her classmate Jimmy for school and church projects, twelve-year-old Sophie must find a way to dispel the boyfriend rumors and to stop the cyberbullying campaign directed against her and a former school bad boy.
    ISBN-13: 978-0-310-71025-7 (softcover)
    ISBN-10: 0-310-71025-1 (softcover)
    [1. Bullying–Fiction. 2. Computers–Fiction. 3. Cliques (Sociology)–Fiction. 4. Schools–Fiction. 5. Christian life–Fiction.] I. Title. II. Series.
PZ7.R88515Sjp 2006
[Fic]–dc22

2005025259

Published in association with the literary agency of Alive Communications, Inc., 7680 Goddard Street, Suite 200, Colorado Springs, CO 80920.

Photography: Synergy Photographic/Brad Lampe
Illustrations: Grace Chen Design & Illustration
Art direction: Merit Alderink
Interior design: Susan Ambs
Interior composition: Ruth Bandstra

Printed in the United States of America

06 07 08 09 10 • 6 5 4 3 2 1

So we fix our eyes not on what is seen, but on what is unseen. For what is seen is temporary, but what is unseen is eternal.

— 2 Corinthians 4:18

Cynthia Cyber, Internet Investigator,

1

leaned toward the computer screen, eyes nearly popping from her head. Could it be that a kid would actually be enough of a bully to print something like THAT for all the middle-school world to see? Impossible — and yet, there it was, a sentence that was already showing its ugly self on computers in bedrooms all over Poquoson, Virginia, and maybe even beyond. It was a sentence that could ravage the social life of its seventh-grade victim before she even checked her email.

"I cannot allow it!" Cynthia Cyber, Internet Investigator, cried. She lunged for the keyboard, fingers already flying—

"It's a seven-passenger van, Little Bit," said a voice from the driver's seat. "You don't have to sit in Jimmy's lap."

Sophie LaCroix jolted back from Sophie-world at several megahertz per second — or something like that. She found herself staring right into Jimmy Wythe's swimming-pool-blue eyes. She had no choice. She really was in his lap.

A round, red spot had formed at the top of each of Jimmy's cheekbones. Sophie was sure her entire *face* was that color.

"Do you want to sit on this side?" Jimmy said as Sophie scrambled her tiny-for-a-twelve-year-old body back into her own seat. "We could trade."

"I don't think that's what she had in mind." Hannah turned around from the van's middle seat in front of them, blinking her eyes against her contact lenses practically at the speed of sound. She was Sophie's inspiration to keep wearing glasses. "Personally, I think seventh grade's a little young to be dating. I know I'm only a year older, but — "

Mrs. Clayton didn't turn around in the front seat, but her trumpet voice blared its way back to them just fine. "There is actually a world of difference between seventh graders and eighth graders."

Yeah, Sophie thought, fanning her still-red face with a folder. *Eighth graders think it's all about the boy-girl thing. I am SO not dating Jimmy Wythe. Or anybody else! EWWW.* She scooted a couple of inches farther away from Jimmy.

It wasn't that Jimmy wasn't a whole lot more decent than most of the boys at Great Marsh Middle School. He was one of the three guys who made films with Sophie and her friends. They didn't make disgusting noises with their armpits and burp the alphabet in the cafeteria — like some other boys she knew. But *date* him — or anybody else?

I do not BELIEVE so!

"So, are you guys going out or what?" Hannah said.

"Not that it's any of your business." Oliver, the eighth grader next to her, gave one of the rubber bands on his braces a snap with his finger. Why, Sophie wondered, did boys have to *do* stuff like that?

"Oh, come on, dish, Little Bit," Coach Nanini said from behind the wheel. He grinned at Sophie in the rearview mirror in that way that always made Sophie think of a big happy gorilla with no hair. She liked to think of him as Coach Virile.

She had to grin back at him.

"We're not going out," Jimmy said. The red spots still punctuated his cheekbones. "We're just, like, friends."

Mrs. Clayton did turn around this time, although her helmet of too-blonde hair didn't move at all. "That's very noble of you, Jimmy, to get Sophie out of the hot seat like that. You're a gentleman."

"Ooh, Mrs. C," Coach Virile said, still grinning. "Don't you know that's the kiss of death for the adolescent male?"

"It's okay," Jimmy said. He pulled his big-from-doing-gymnastics shoulders all the way up to his now-very-red ears. "It's what my dad's teaching me to be."

"Bravo," Mrs. Clayton said. "I'd like to bring him in and have him train the entire male population of the school."

Coach Virile's voice went up even higher than it usually did, which was pretty squeaky for a guy whose beefy arms stuck out from both sides of the driver's seat. "I thought I was doing that, Mrs. C."

"I wish you'd step it up a little," she said.

Sophie glanced sideways at Jimmy, who was currently ducking his head of short-cropped, sun-blond hair. *I guess he is kind of a gentleman*, Sophie thought. She had never heard him imitate her high-pitched voice like those Fruit Loop boys did, or seen him knock some girl's pencil off her desk just to be obnoxious. And somehow he managed to be pretty nice and still cool at the same time. The Corn Pops definitely thought so. The we-have-everything girls were always chasing after him.

"So if you're not going out," Hannah said, "why were you in his lap?"

She was turned all the way around now, arms resting on the back of her seat as if she were going to spend the rest of the trip from Richmond exploring the topic. Oliver groaned.

"Inquiring minds want to know," Hannah said.

NOSY minds, you mean, Sophie thought. But she sighed and said, "I wasn't really sitting in his lap. Well, I was, only that wasn't my plan. I didn't even know I was doing it, because I was being — well, somebody else — and Jimmy's window was a computer screen — all our stuff's piled up and blocking my window so I couldn't use it — anyway, it all started with the conference. I really got into it."

Coach Virile laughed, spattering the windshield. "We can always count on you to be honest, Little Bit."

"Let me get this straight," said Oliver. "You were pretending to be, like, some imaginary person?"

"More like a character for our next film."

Jimmy, still blotchy, nodded. "For Film Club. Sophie always comes up with the main character."

"I play around with it some before I tell the whole group," Sophie said. "I try not to get too carried away with it in school." She didn't add that if she got in trouble for daydreaming, her father would take away her movie camera.

"Ya think?" Hannah said. She put on her serious face. "A little advice: don't tell that to a whole lot of people at Great Marsh. You'd be committing social suicide."

"Especially don't let it get out on the Internet," Oliver said. "Everybody'll think you're weird."

"I *am* weird," Sophie said. "Well, unique. Who isn't?" That was the motto of Sophie and her friends, the Corn Flakes: Keep the power God gives you to be yourself.

"I may be weird," Hannah said, "but I do *not* go around acting out imaginary characters, okay?"

You wouldn't be very good at it, Sophie thought. She ran an elfin hand through her short wedge of honey-colored hair and squinted her brown eyes through her glasses.

"What?" Hannah said.

"Well," Sophie said slowly, "you might not be unique in that way, but you are somehow. Everybody is."

Hannah's eyebrows twitched. "I try not to let that get out. I'd like to get through middle school without being the punch line of everybody's jokes, thank you very much."

"Speaking of bullying." Coach Virile cleared his throat.

"Yes," Mrs. Clayton said. "What did you glean from the conference?"

"Can I 'glean' if I don't know what it means?" Oliver said.

"It means what did we learn," Sophie said. It came in handy to have a best-best friend who almost knew the whole dictionary. Fiona, she knew, would be proud.

Hannah gave Oliver a poke. "So what did you glean, genius?"

Oliver held up his folder, which had the shield of the Commonwealth of Virginia on it, and the words "Governor's Conference on Cyber Bullying." He flipped it open and read, "'Seventeen million children in America use the Internet. Twenty to thirty percent of them report being victims of bullying through email, instant messaging, chat rooms, websites, online diaries, and cell phone text messages.'"

Sophie hadn't remembered any of that. She'd been way wrapped up in the stories actual kids told, right from the stage, about how people had written heinous things about them on the Internet (*heinous* was one of Fiona's best words, meaning worse than awful) and everybody believed them. One victim changed schools. Another one refused to even go to school. And there was actually a boy who fought back with his own website and got suspended for the rest of the year while the original bullies were never caught.

Cynthia Cyber was outraged. This could not be allowed to go on! Fortunately she had taken on the job of Internet Investigator, ready to do battle to clean up cyberspace—

"Are you doing that imaginary character thing right now?" Hannah said.

Sophie froze and looked at her hand, which was poised in the air, fingers curled around a not-there computer mouse.

"Yeah, she's doing it," Jimmy said. He gave Sophie a shy smile. She noticed his teeth were as straight as slats in a fence.

"You can't tell me you two aren't going out," Hannah said.

"All right, Round Table," Mrs. Clayton said. "Let's stay focused."

Yeah, can we please? Sophie thought. Sometimes she wondered if Hannah and Oliver even took Round Table seriously. *She* definitely did. After all, the four of them, plus Mrs. Clayton and Coach Virile and a few other teachers, were the group that was trying to stop bullying at Great Marsh Middle School by teaching kids how to treat each other and helping bullies be better people instead of just punishing them. To Sophie, it was an awesome responsibility, which was why she had spent the whole day at the conference in Richmond figuring out how the Round Table could help stop an even worse kind of bullying—the stuff that happened on people's computers.

"How about you, Jimbo?" Coach Virile said.

"I know what *Jimbo* was thinking about," Hannah muttered.

"Uh—that cyber bullying is simple," Jimmy said. "Like, all you have to know is how to log on to the Internet, and do email and get in chat rooms, and download stuff."

"Which is why it's spreading like a wildfire," Mrs. Clayton said. She shot the two back seats a bullet-eyed look. "And since there's no adult supervision on the Internet, it's up to you kids to stop it."

"Not just you four," Coach Virile said. "But you're the leaders."

Oliver snapped both sets of rubber bands. Sophie rolled her eyes at Jimmy, who rolled his back.

"I don't see how we're gonna stop it," Oliver said. "It's all under the adult radar, like you said, so people hardly ever get caught. Not like when they do regular bullying at school."

"We adults definitely have to do our part," Mrs. Clayton said. "I have absolutely no online life. I'm going to have to get hip to this Internet thing."

Oliver snorted, and Hannah covered her whole face with her hands. As Sophie turned to grin at Jimmy, she saw in the rearview mirror that even Coach Virile's eyes were twinkling.

"I'm so glad you're all amused," Mrs. Clayton said.

"What about you, Little Bit?" Coach Nanini said. "What did you learn?"

That Cynthia Cyber is going to kick buns as an Internet investigator, Sophie thought. But she gave Hannah a being-careful look and instead said, "It seems like the first thing to do is keep trying to get kids to stop treating each other like enemies so cyber bullying won't happen in the first place."

"Good luck," Hannah said.

"We *are* having good luck with that, though," Coach Virile said. "For just about every student who's come before Round Table, we've been able to get some change going."

"Except that one fat kid," Oliver said.

Mrs. Clayton shot him another bullet look.

"Sorry. That poor overweight kid that ripped off Sophie's — "

"Eddie Wornom," Coach said.

At the sound of that name, Sophie shivered. Stealing wasn't the only thing Eddie had done to her since she met him back in sixth grade. Even working with Coach Virile on Campus Commission hadn't changed Eddie, except to make him worse. He was away at military school now, and that was fine with Sophie.

"It would take a miracle to rehabilitate Eddie," Jimmy whispered to Sophie.

"Yeah," Sophie said. "That would be right up there with the loaves and fishes."

Jimmy laughed from someplace way down in his throat. "If Eddie had been at the loaves and fishes, there still wouldn't have been enough food to go around."

"You know it."

They settled into a comfortable silence. It occurred to Sophie that she had started out that morning wishing her Corn Flakes were with her — Willoughby and Maggie and Darbie and Kitty and especially Fiona. She had missed them some during the day, like when she went to the restroom and there was nobody to giggle with. Hannah wasn't a giggler.

But most of the time she and Jimmy had talked — more than they did when the other Lucky Charms, Vincent and Nathan, were around.

But for Pete's sake, Sophie thought now, *why does Hannah think we're going out? Like Mama and Daddy would let me, even if I wanted to.*

Besides, Sophie could never figure out where seventh-grade couples "went" when they were "going out." Yikes. They were *twelve.*

"All right, Round Table," Mrs. Clayton said. "You have an assignment."

"Is it a lot?" Hannah said. "I'm going to have a ton of home-work from missing the whole day today."

"You'll manage," Mrs. Clayton said. "Before we meet next Monday, I want each of you to come up with some ideas for put-ting the things we learned at the conference to work in our own anti-bullying campaign."

Sophie smiled what she knew was her wispy smile. She was already coming up with a film they would show to the whole school, starring Cynthia Cyber —

"What time is it?" Hannah said as they pulled into the school driveway.

"Three-thirty," Coach Nanini said. "You can still catch the late bus."

"There's a line out there for it already." Hannah sighed loudly. "I hate it when it's so crowded. Everybody that's been playing sports smells the whole bus up."

"Well, excuse them for perspiring," Oliver said.

Once again, Sophie and Jimmy rolled their eyes at each other. *It was almost as much fun rolling them with him as it was rolling them with the Flakes*, Sophie thought.

"I think somebody's trying to get your attention, Little Bit," Coach Virile said, pointing through the windshield.

Sophie grinned. It was hard to miss Willoughby, who was waving both of her red-and-white-and-blue pom-poms and yelling, "SO-Phee!" in her biggest cheerleader voice.

"How does all that sound come out of that little person?" Coach said.

Although Willoughby wasn't quite as small as Sophie, she was still petite, and looked even more so under her mop of darkish, wavy hair that was even now springing out of its clips as she bounced up and down shouting at Sophie.

Sophie called good-bye to everybody in the van even as she wriggled her way through the line to Willoughby. When Sophie reached her, Willoughby grabbed her by the sleeve and dragged her away from the stream of kids waiting for the late bus.

"You aren't going to *believe* this," Willoughby said instead of "hello." Her very round hazel eyes were bright with excitement. "We've been dying to tell you all day, and I told the rest of the Flakes I'd tell you since I was the only one staying after school and we figured you'd be back to catch the late bus —"

"What *is* it?" Sophie said. Sometimes Willoughby's thoughts went as wild as her hair.

"You will never guess who's coming back to school."

"Who?"

Willoughby sucked in a huge breath. "Eddie Wornom," she said.

"No WAY!" Sophie shook her head. "He's at military school."

"Not anymore. At least that's what B.J. and Cassie were saying in fifth period."

Sophie let out a relieved sigh. "You know you can't trust a Corn Pop. They're just trying to scare you."

Willoughby's eyes were as big as Frisbees. "You think?"

"I *know*. What do the Pops do better than anything else?"

"Put on lip gloss?"

"Besides that."

Willoughby nodded slowly. "Spread rumors."

"Exactly." Sophie gave Willoughby a quick hug around the neck. "We have to just ignore stuff like that. They said that at the conference, which I wanna tell you all about, only I've gotta go."

"IM me tonight," Willoughby said.

"You coming or what?" the bus driver yelled.

Sophie scrambled up the steps and hurled herself into an empty seat just as the door sighed shut and the bus lurched around the curve in the driveway. Sophie lurched with it, rocking into the person next to her.

She looked up into the eyes of Eddie Wornom.

Sophie pulled back and stared. She'd thought it was Eddie. It was Eddie's

2

sandy-blond-with-bangs hair and matching almost-invisible eyebrows. But this guy's hair was way shorter than Eddie's. And the cheeks weren't Eddie's pudgy ones, and the mouth wasn't curled up and poised for some lame remark like, "Hey, Soapy. When's the breast fairy gonna come visit you?"

This kid was taller than Eddie. She could tell that even though he was sitting down. He was also thinner. And he didn't look like he was capable of burping the alphabet. Sophie could see his now-sticking-out Adam's apple move up and down.

"Hi, Sophie."

Sophie jerked back like a startled rabbit. How was Eddie Wornom's voice coming out of this kid's mouth? This kid who didn't say it like he wanted to hurl at the same time?

"Do I know you?" Sophie said.

"Uh, yeah," he said.

It *was* Eddie. What was he doing on the bus when he hadn't even started back to classes yet? *He's probably just here to torment me*, Sophie thought. She clutched the edge of the seat and waited for what was sure to come. Something from the you-sure-didn't-get-any-brains-while-I-was-gone department.

Eddie swallowed again. It looked like it hurt. "Everybody says I look really different," he said.

Sophie could only stare. And think of all the other times she'd been this close to Eddie Wornom. Every one of those times, she'd felt like she was either going to throw up from gross out or pass out from terror.

The bus lurched again, this time at its first stop. As a clump of kids gathered at the door, Sophie popped up and tore down the aisle toward the back, looking for a familiar face. After all, it was only a matter of time before Eddie went Fruit Loop on her, she was sure of that.

When she spotted two of the Wheaties, she dived into their seat and hissed, "Scoot over! Please!"

The Wheaties were a group of soccer-playing and every-other-kind-of-ball-playing girls the Corn Flakes got along with. They were very un-Corn Pop and very cool.

"What's up?" said Gill, the bigger of the two. A couple of straggly strands of her lanky red hair trailed out from under the blue toboggan cap she wore pulled down to her eyebrows. Beside her, by the window, her friend Harley grunted, which was all she usually did, since Gill did most of the talking. Harley just smiled a lot under the brim of her Redskins ball cap, until her cheeks came up to her eyes and squinted them closed.

"I got stuck sitting next to Eddie Wornom!" Sophie whispered. Harley grunted again.

"I thought he was gone," Gill said.

"I guess he's back." Sophie looked furtively up the aisle to the seat she'd just vacated. "For once, B.J. and them weren't lying."

Both Gill and Harley grunted this time. The Corn Flakes had never told the Wheaties that they called the popular girls Corn Pops, but they knew the Wheaties didn't like the Pops any more than they did.

"It's in our Code not to put them down just because they do it to us," the Corn Flakes had told the Wheaties more than once. But it wasn't easy for any of them.

"Where is he?" Gill said.

"Second row back on the other side," Sophie said.

Gill rose up out of the seat just far enough to keep from getting yelled at by the bus driver and shook her head. "That kid isn't fat enough to be Eddie Wornom."

"I guess he lost weight," Sophie said. "What's he doing now? I can't see."

Gill craned her neck. "He's got Tod Ravelli sitting with him. Colton Messik's behind them. The Three Stooges."

The three Fruit Loops, Sophie thought, groaning inside. "What are they doing?"

"Tod's all up in Eddie's dental work, tellin' him something. Colton's clapping like an ape."

"What about Eddie?"

"He's not saying anything — for once."

Harley grunted. She too was up on her knees, watching.

"What?" Sophie said.

Gill looked at Harley, and they both nodded. "We think Eddie's smiling too big," Gill said. "It's like he's straining his mouth or something."

"Just wait ten seconds," Sophie said miserably. "He'll start yelling swear words."

"That's all he knows," Gill said.

A block later, the first two seats erupted with snorts and too-loud laughs that clearly said *we're ripping somebody apart up here*. Sophie could almost see herself being shoved into a trash can, or worse.

When the bus stopped at the corner of Odd Road where Sophie lived, she scooted hurriedly past the Fruit Loops without even glancing at them. She definitely didn't look up from the sidewalk as the bus pulled away. She was sure she would have seen Eddie hanging out, waggling his tongue.

There was only one thing to do, and that was to get online *immediately* and find out what the rest of the Flakes knew. Fiona, Darbie, and Sophie were in different classes than Maggie and Willoughby for some periods, so Fiona and Darbie might have heard different things. Julia and Anne-Stuart were the Pops in their section, and although they didn't talk as loud as B.J. and Cassie, they were the ones who decided what rumors were spread and how.

But Sophie headed for the family room to check on Mama first. She was enthroned on the couch, hands folded over her pregnant tummy, dozing in front of the TV with the sound muted. Sophie watched her for a minute.

Everybody always said Mama and Sophie looked alike with their wispy smiles and round brown eyes and pixie-like bodies. But lately Mama didn't even look like herself, much less like Sophie. Everything about her was puffy — not just her tummy. And her usually bouncy, highlighted-to-cover-gray curls were pulled up into an untidy bun on the top of her head so it didn't get ratty from lying down all the time.

The doctor had told Mama she had to remain completely off her feet if Baby Girl LaCroix was going to stay put until it was time for her to be born in March. Being inside the house made Mama milky-pale, and not being involved in absolutely everything Sophie and her older sister, Lacie, and her little brother, Zeke, did kept the wispy smile from appearing as often as it used to.

Since this was only December, Mama still had a lot more time to spend, as she put it, being a beached whale. As Sophie watched the air puff out between Mama's lips in sleep, she felt a wave of I-need-to-do-more-to-cheer-her-up.

Right after I check my email I'm going to bring her a snack, Sophie thought. *Peanut butter and celery, with honey for dipping—*

She was about to turn and tiptoe out when Mama's eyes fluttered open and she gave Sophie a swollen smile.

"Hey, Dream Girl," she said. "How was the conference? I want to hear everything." She struggled to sit up. "Not that I would understand any of it. You know I'm computer challenged."

"That's okay." Sophie dropped her backpack on the floor and hurried to adjust Mama's pillows. "You do a lot of other stuff really well."

"Not these days," Mama said. She fluttered a hand toward the covered basket beside the couch. "And if I even look at a pair of knitting needles again, I'll probably poke somebody with them."

Sophie nodded. The basket was overflowing with sweaters and booties and blankets for Baby Girl LaCroix that Mama had knitted and knitted until two nights ago when she said she was sick of the sight of yarn and wanted to put the whole pile down the garbage disposal. Daddy had rescued it and carried Mama upstairs to bed.

Sophie sniffed the air, but she didn't smell supper. "Where's Lacie?"

"She has the night off from cooking," Mama said. "Daddy's bringing home Chinese."

"Yes!" Sophie said. Not only did she love egg rolls, and moo-goo-gai-pan because it was fun to say, but this meant she didn't have to help in the kitchen, and there would be more time to find out stuff from the Flakes. She edged toward the door.

"Why don't you go do your thing?" Mama said. "You can tell all of us about the conference over chow mein. I'll send Zeke up when Daddy gets here."

Sophie was glad Zeke was with Fiona's grandfather Boppa. A lot of the time, *she* had to watch him after school, which meant endless hours playing Spider-Man.

"Love you," Sophie said as she backed toward the stairs.

"Love you more," Mama said and closed her eyes again.

Sophie flew to her room and turned on her computer. It had been Daddy's at one time, and when he had given it to her, he'd built a special desk for it so she could have more privacy in their busy house. It had been kind of a reward for taking more responsibility helping with Mama. It didn't exactly go with the flowy chiffon curtains Mama had hung around Sophie's bed or the princess lamp on the table that had given light to so many of Sophie's daydreams, but that didn't matter. Right now Cynthia Cyber, Internet Investigator, had work to do —

I have to stay focused on the real world right now, Sophie told herself as she clicked on the Internet icon. And Eddie Wornom was about as real as this world got.

Sure enough, there was a group email from Fiona — WORD-GIRL — to all the Flakes. The subject was EDDIE WORNOM ALERT!!!!

IT'S OFFICIAL, CORN FLAKES, Fiona had written, EDDIE WORNOM IS COMING BACK TO GREAT

MARSH MIDDLE SCHOOL. HEARD JULIA AND ANNE-STUART TALKING ABOUT IT 5TH. ASKED COACH YATES ABOUT IT 6TH. SHE SAID HE WAS IN THE OFFICE ALL AFTERNOON AND THE SCHOOL'S GIVING HIM ANOTHER CHANCE. WE HAVE TO BE VIGILANT. IT COULD GET UGLY.

Sophie was just reaching for the dictionary to look up *vigilant* when an instant message popped up. It was from IRISH. Because Darbie was from Northern Ireland, she used IRISH for just about everything.

IRISH: *I won't believe that blackguard is back.*

Sophie could almost hear Darbie saying that in her lilty Irish voice. She always pronounced *blackguard*, another word for absurd little creep, like *blaggard*.

DREAMGRL: *He IS back!!!! I saw him on the late bus.*
IRISH: *Evil!*

Before Sophie could answer, another IM popped up, this time from Kitty. Nobody IM'd and emailed more than Kitty. Because of her leukemia and the chemotherapy that made her sick, she was being homeschooled. The Internet kept her from feeling like she was missing absolutely everything.

MEOW: *Hi, Sophie.*
DREAMGRL: *Hi, Kitty. Did you hear about Eddie?*
MEOW: *Yes! for once I'm glad I'm not at school!*
                     LOL!!!

It had taken Sophie a while to learn that LOL meant "laugh out loud." Now that she could spend more time online, she was getting the language down.

DREAMGRL: *I SAW him*
MEOW: *Eddie?*
DREAMGRL: *Yes. On the late bus*

MEOW:	*was he mean?*

Sophie grabbed a hunk of her hair and toyed with its blunt-cut ends. She had to decide what to say next so she didn't break Corn Flake Code. It was hard when you were talking about the most heinous boy on the planet.

MEOW:	*Did he cuss on the bus?*
DREAMGRL:	*No*
MEOW:	*Belch?*
DREAMGRL:	*Nope*
MEOW:	*Was he even awake? LOL*
DREAMGRL:	*LOL!!!*

Sophie paused. It would be okay to just state a fact, right?

DREAMGRL:	*He isn't as fat as he used to be.*
MEOW:	*POS*

Sophie definitely knew that code. *POS* meant "parent over shoulder." When you saw that, you really had to be careful about what you wrote. Sophie was glad she didn't have that problem anymore, like she did when she'd had to use the computer down in Daddy's study. There was *always* POS going on back then.

Cynthia Cyber squinted through her glasses at the screen. She was instantly alert when she saw POS. That could mean bullying was happening that a kid didn't want a mom or dad to know about. She cupped her hand on her mouse, finger ready to click on anything heinous that might flash before her —

The bell sound announced another instant message. It was from Go4Gold. It took Sophie a second to realize that was Jimmy.

Go4Gold:	*Sophie?*
DREAMGRL:	*Hi, Jimmy.*
Go4Gold:	*I have an idea for what Mrs C told us to do.*
DREAMGRL:	*For Round Table?*

GO4Gold:	Ya. Wanna meet before school tomorrow?
DREAMGRL:	Where?
GO4Gold:	Library. 7:30?
DREAMGRL:	I'm there.

"SO phcc! SUP-per!"

Something banged against the door, as if someone had thrown a bag of potatoes at it. Sophie knew it was Zeke, probably trying to launch himself up onto the doorframe so he could climb down like Spider-Man. Meanwhile, bells were dinging on the computer.

IRISH:	You still there?
MEOW:	Where did you go?
Go4Gold:	See ya tomorrow
DREAMGRL:	Gotta go eat

Sophie clicked offline and gave an impatient sigh. When Sophie slid onto her cushion at the big square coffee table in the family room, Daddy was tapping chopsticks against her plate. Never a good sign.

"We're not interfering with your busy schedule, are we, Soph?" he said.

There was just enough of a gleam in his dark blue eyes to tell Sophie she wasn't in the penalty box yet. That was what Daddy called it when they were in real trouble. He talked about everything like it was a sports event.

"Sorry. I just had to log off," Sophie said.

"Could you stay off for about seven seconds after supper?" Lacie said. "I have to look something up for my history paper."

Daddy looked from Lacie, with her dark hair and her intense eyes, back to Sophie. "You two aren't going to start fighting over Net time, are you?" he said.

"We're not fighting," Lacie said. She gave Sophie a work-with-me-here smile and nodded so definitely toward Mama her ponytail jerked.

Sophie got it. These days Lacie always made sure they didn't do anything to upset Mama. Sophie knew her mother would never actually poke somebody with a knitting needle, but being pregnant did seem to make a person very emotional.

"We're just working out the schedule," Lacie said to Daddy.

"Take all the time you need," Sophie said, smiling hard. "Just let me know when you're off."

Daddy bunched his eyebrows at Sophie again. "So you can get on to do homework, I assume."

Sophie stifled a sigh. Every time she thought she and Daddy were going to get along forever, he did something new to make her want to take her moo-goo-gai-pan and eat it in the closet.

"So!" Mama said. She dunked an egg roll into the sweet-and-sour sauce with one hand while she pushed the fortune cookies out of Zeke's reach with the other. "Tell us about the cyber-bullying conference, Sophie."

"Spider bullying?" Zeke said with a chow mein noodle hanging out of his mouth.

Lacie gave him a lesson in *cyber* versus *spider* while Sophie told Mama and Daddy about the conference. When she was through, both their brows were puckered like she had the flu and they were deciding whether to call the doctor. Sophie held her breath.

"That's a real eye-opener," Daddy said. He ran a big hand over his hair, which went in several different directions just the way Zeke's did. "But it makes sense. You kids are the constantly connected generation. You always have to be IM'ing or emailing or chatting—"

"Or talking on a cell phone." Lacie smiled so sweetly Sophie was surprised sugar didn't collect on her lips. It didn't work on Daddy.

"Forget it, Lace," he said. "No cell phone."

"That's it," Lacie said, still grinning. "My life is over."

Sophie had to admit that if anybody deserved a cell phone, it was Lacie. She made straight A's and was freshman class president at the high school and played every sport, *and* she did a lot of the cooking and took turns with Sophie watching Zeke now that Mama had to stay down. She was also in the church youth group, where she had learned not to be a complete snot about all of that, especially to Sophie. Sophie thanked Jesus for that every day.

"Sounds like I better get more in the loop on this cyber stuff," Daddy said.

Sophie wondered if that was the same as getting hip. And then she squirmed. She wasn't sure she wanted her father in her loop. But he was watching her as if he could see into her brain.

"I brought home a bunch of stuff for parents," she forced herself to say. "It's in my folder."

Daddy smothered the top of Sophie's head with his hand. "Way to be a team player, Soph," he said. "Any other kid would've destroyed anything that would let parents invade their world."

Sophie wriggled out from under his hand. "Nobody I talk to online is bullying," she said. She didn't add that she was *very* glad not to have POS going on. "Since I'm so wonderful, could you give me a ride to school tomorrow at seven-fifteen?"

"Why—do you have a date?"

"Rusty!" Mama said.

Daddy held up his palm. "Kidding. Just kidding."

On IM, Cynthia Cyber thought, *that would be KJK*.

Sophie wisped a secret smile. If Jimmy was thinking what she was thinking, Cynthia was about to become a star.

Sophie worked at staying out of Cynthia-world

3

the next morning as her footsteps echoed in the still-empty halls on the way to the school library. Round Table was serious stuff, and she wanted to be sharp. There would be time enough for Cynthia Cyber when she and Jimmy started planning their movie. Cynthia would, of course, be perfect as the main character, and Fiona could be her personal assistant—

Jimmy was waiting for her at one of the tables, looking just-showered with his blond hair still in wet spikes. He looked sort of soft, like Zeke did right after he woke up, and before he started squalling that he wouldn't eat a pancake unless it was shaped like a superhero.

"Hi," Sophie said.

Jimmy jumped up and pulled out a chair for her, and then glanced around like he was making sure nobody had seen him. Sophie didn't blame him. The Fruit Loops could work with that for days. *Especially with Eddie back*, she thought.

She sat down and raised her eyebrows at Jimmy.

"So, my idea," he said. His voice was morning-husky. "I think Round Table should do a website. Y' know, like, on cyber bullying."

"Oh...," Sophie said. She could practically see Cynthia snapping her face from the computer monitor to stare.

The two red spots reappeared at the tops of Jimmy's cheeks. "You hate it."

"I don't hate it," Sophie said slowly. "I just thought — "

She stopped. Jimmy looked like someone was about to kick him in his very-straight teeth.

"It's just that I don't know how to do a website," she said.

Jimmy sprang into a smile. "Oh — well, me neither. Somebody else — like Mrs. Britt — would have to design it. We'd just give her ideas."

"Mrs. Britt? The computer lady?"

"Yeah. Vincent says she's, like, this genius."

Sophie nodded. Vincent would know. He spent as much time exploring websites as the Flakes did emailing each other. Vincent sometimes had a dazed look, like he'd gotten lost in there somewhere.

Still, it wasn't a movie.

"I have some ideas," Jimmy said. "And since you're creative, you could probably come up with some too." He shrugged like he couldn't think of anything else to say.

Sophie was squirmy. "I don't visit websites that much. Y' know, Fiona usually does the research for our films, she and Darbie and Vincent — "

"Maybe we could still use your character you were thinking up yesterday."

Sophie pushed her glasses up with her finger. "You mean, like, Cynthia Cyber could be on a website?"

"Sure. Who is she?"

"Internet Investigator."

"Sweet."

It was suddenly Christmas morning on Jimmy's face, so Sophie tried not to sag in her seat. Making a website wouldn't be the same as being Cynthia Cyber in a movie —

Springing up from her desk chair, she raised both hands in the air. Victory — she had tracked the cyber bullies straight to their email address.

"You okay?" Jimmy said.

"Yeah," Sophie lied.

Jimmy reached for his backpack, fumbled with it, and dumped half the contents onto the table. A granola bar slid into Sophie's lap.

"I brought that for you anyway," Jimmy said. There were two more red spots on each cheek. He practically buried his head in the backpack and emerged with a piece of paper and a pencil. "I'll write stuff down," he said.

Sophie had to giggle. "You can be Maggie." Maggie always kept records in the Treasure Book of everything for Corn Flakes Productions and Film Club. "You don't *look* like Maggie," she said. "I mean, like, she's a girl and you're a boy — "

"I'm glad you see that," Jimmy said.

Sophie stuffed her hand over her mouth so she wouldn't guffaw the librarian out of her office.

"Okay," Jimmy said. "We could have, like, a quiz that people could take to see if they're bullying or being bullied."

Sophie tugged at a short strand of hair. "So — what would Cynthia Cyber do?"

"She could tell how to score it."

"Oh," Sophie said. "So there would just be a picture of her or something?"

"No," Jimmy said. "She could talk and move her head and stuff."

"Like a little mini-movie?"

Jimmy bobbed his head so hard, Sophie found herself nodding too.

"Okay," she said. "I guess you could write that down."

"I could write down that if somebody scores in the cyberbully range, Cynthia Cyber gets, like, huge and covers the whole screen and her nostrils go all big — "

"And she gets laser eyes," Sophie said.

Okay, so maybe this wouldn't be so bad.

The warning bell rang, and Jimmy scowled at it.

"Man, we were just getting started."

"You started on something without us?" said a familiar voice behind them.

Sophie turned and smiled at Fiona, who had Nathan and Vincent and the other Corn Flakes behind her. Fiona didn't exactly smile back. She craned her neck toward the paper on the table. Sophie wondered if that could be called FOS, "friend over shoulder."

"What's up, dude?" Vincent said, his voice cracking.

He punched Jimmy on the arm. It was such a boy-thing, one of the many reasons Sophie was glad she was a girl. Willoughby came up behind her and hugged her neck.

"Are you planning a movie without us?" Maggie shook her head, splashing her dark silky bob against her cheeks. "I don't think you can do that." Maggie's voice was solid and square like the rest of her. If you wanted to know what the rules were, you only had to ask Maggie.

"It's not a film." Fiona's shiny gray eyes swept across Jimmy's notes. "It's a website."

"We don't do websites," Maggie said.

Fiona gave a sniff and tossed aside the wayward strand of straight, deep brown hair that fell over one eye. "It doesn't look like *we* are doing it."

Nathan punched Jimmy on the other arm. Then his face turned red beneath his mop of curly hair. That was mostly how he communicated.

"What's the deal, man?" Vincent said.

Jimmy looked at Sophie, who looked up at the group. "We have to do a project for Round Table," she said.

Darbie perched her slender long-legged self on the edge of the table and tapped the paper. Sophie couldn't see her face because her reddish hair fell forward, but she had a feeling Darbie wasn't smiling, either.

"It's a website?" Darbie said.

"On cyber bullying," Sophie said.

Fiona folded her arms. "No offense," she said, "but neither one of you knows anything about designing a website."

"I know," Sophie said, "so we're going to get Mrs. Britt to help us — "

"Mrs. Britt? What about us?" Fiona's big eyes got bigger. "Hello — Vincent's king of the computer geeks. I have a program that shows you how to make websites — I was gonna surprise you with one for the Corn — for us."

"I didn't even know you liked websites, Sophie," Darbie said.

Even her pronouncing it "Soophie" the way she always did didn't make her sound any friendlier at the moment, as far as Sophie was concerned. She looked at each of them, with their arms folded and their eyes all slit-like. Willoughby was wrapping a curl around her finger so tight it was turning blue.

"She *doesn't* care about websites," Maggie said. "Neither do I. I don't even have a computer at home."

It doesn't have anything to do with you! Sophie thought.

But she didn't say it. After all, she never did anything that didn't have *something* to do with them.

Sophie looked at Fiona, whose magic gray eyes were obviously waiting for something. Sophie just wasn't sure what. Thankfully the second warning bell rang. Sophie dived for her backpack, banging her forehead on the table.

"You okay?" Jimmy said.

"Uh-huh," Sophie said.

"Here." Jimmy held out her backpack. Sophie took it, smiled, and ran.

There was no time to talk to Darbie and Fiona during their first-and-second-period language arts/social studies block. But the minute the bell rang and they were headed for third-period PE, Darbie was all over Sophie in the hall.

"You okay, Sophie?" she said in a voice that sounded suspiciously like Jimmy's. Her dark eyes were dancing. "Let me get that backpack for you." She flexed her arm muscles.

Sophie rolled her eyes at her and glanced nervously at Fiona. Her eyes were *not* dancing, and that prickled up the back of Sophie's neck. "Oh, thank you, darling," Sophie said to Darbie, in a voice she hoped sounded like a romance novel.

Willoughby hurried up to them, dragging Maggie behind her. Even her hair was in exclamation points.

"I know you can't have a boyfriend, Sophie," she said. "But Jimmy really *likes* you!"

"Not only *can't* I have a boyfriend," Sophie said, "I don't *want* a boyfriend."

"That's a good thing," somebody said, "because you'll never *get* one."

Sophie didn't have to turn around to know it was Julia Cummings, queen of the Corn Pops. Julia sailed past, thick auburn hair swishing across her shoulders. She didn't look at Sophie, either, but Anne-Stuart, Julia's second-in-command, cast Sophie a watery-eyed look and sniffed. Sophie had never seen skinny, everything-pale Anne-Stuart when she didn't need a tissue.

"You know that isn't true, Sophie," Willoughby said when the Pops were gone. "You could *so* have Jimmy for a boyfriend if you wanted one."

"I *don't* want one!" Sophie cried.

Darbie's eyes sparked mischief.

"But the Corn Pops don't know that, do they?" she said.

Willoughby's eyes grew to dinner plate size. "You mean we're going to make them think Jimmy and Sophie are going out?"

"That would be lying." Maggie looked at Sophie. "Wouldn't it?"

They *all*, even Fiona, looked at Sophie, who grinned at the image in her mind of the Corn Pops with their mouths hanging open like chimpanzees because they believed their favorite target had a boyfriend.

"We would just be playing," Sophie said finally.

"And if they can't figure that out," Darbie said, "that's their problem."

They stopped outside the girls' locker-room door.

"Is everybody in?" Darbie said.

"I'm not gonna do it," Maggie said. "But I won't give it away."

Willoughby gave one of her shrieks that always sounded to Sophie like a poodle yelping. "I probably won't be able to stop laughing."

Fiona arched an eyebrow at her. "So what else is new?"

"B.J. and Cassie are behind us," Darbie whispered.

Fiona put her lips close to Sophie's ear. "You don't really like Jimmy, do you? I mean, boyfriend-girlfriend?"

"No!" Sophie said. *"Ewww!"*

Fiona knotted up her pink rosebud of a mouth. "It really would be excellent to freak out the Corn Pops—it wouldn't be mean."

"Hurry up!" Darbie whispered.

Fiona's eyes took on their magic shine. "Come on, Soph, dish," she said in a too-loud voice. They pushed through the door and headed for their locker row. "Did Jimmy ask you out or not?"

Sophie's prickles disappeared. "I'll never tell," she said. Her voice squeaked, which it always did when she was about to give way to giggles. Willoughby already had.

"He's a fine bit of stuff, Sophie," Darbie said.

"What's that mean?" Maggie said.

"It means he's a hottie," Fiona said as she twirled the dial on her lock. "Right, Soph?"

"Total hottie," Sophie said.

Several lockers down, Julia laughed and fluffed her hair out of the neck of the GMMS T-shirt she'd just pulled over her head.

"Like she even knows what a hottie is," Cassie said in a coarse whisper. She rolled her close-together eyes.

Fiona winked at Sophie over the top of her open locker door. "Come on, Soph. Tell us how you feel about him."

"We're your best friends," Willoughby said, and then buried her face in her wadded-up sweater.

Sophie gave an elaborate sigh. "All right, if you must know . . ."

All of the Flakes, including Maggie, leaned toward her. Sophie sneaked a glance at the Pops. Their bodies were tilted in her direction too.

"Well?" Fiona said.

"Sophie, we're desperate to know," Darbie said.

Sophie closed her eyes and tried to remember something she'd heard on the soap opera Mama watched when she was really bored. If they were going to drive the Corn Pops nuts, she had to be convincing.

"I think . . . ," she said.

Corn Flake heads nodded.

"No, I don't think—I *know*—it's real this time." Sophie put her hand on her chest. "I'm in love."

Willoughby gave the poodle shriek. The bell rang for roll check. The Pops pushed past them, faces looking ready to burst like water balloons.

When they were gone, the Corn Flakes jumped up into one big high five.

"We got them," Sophie cried.

Fiona smacked her palm twice. "We got them *good*!"

They were still laughing when they reached the gym and staggered into their roll-check line. The Corn Pops, in the next line over, stared at Sophie, lower lips hanging, just the way Sophie had imagined. And then Julia moved hers.

"Hey, Sophie," she said.

Sophie was a little surprised. That was the second time today Julia had said something to her. Ever since the Pops had been kicked off the cheerleading squad for being mean, they barely spoke to the Flakes. They knew if they bullied the Corn Flakes at all, they would be suspended forever.

"I just want to say something," Julia said.

Sophie shrugged. "So say it."

Behind her, Darbie whispered, "Look out. She's wretched because Jimmy likes you and not her."

"And you can't go running to the Tattletale Table." Julia flung her hair over her shoulder with her head. "Because I'm just expressing my opinion."

"It's a free country," B.J. put in. She narrowed her eyes below her buttery-blonde bangs so hard that her pudgy cheeks drew upward.

Julia gave the hair another fling. "I just don't think it's fair that you and Jimmy Wythe are the only seventh graders that got to go to that conference. Tod is class *president*, and *I'm* vice president. We're, like, the *real* leaders of the class."

"Coach Yates alert," Cassie said between clenched teeth.

Behind Julia, Anne-Stuart snapped a cell phone closed and stuffed it in the pocket of her hoodie. Julia handed hers off to Cassie, who stuck it in the elastic of her track pants.

"It seems like you're trying to take everything away from us," Julia said.

Sophie would have felt sorry for her if Julia's eyes hadn't clearly said what her mouth didn't: *but you just aren't cool enough, Sophie LaCroix.*

So Sophie shrugged again. "I'm not trying to take anything away from you. Honest. You don't have anything I want."

While Julia was still blinking at her, Sophie knelt down and retied her shoe. Within a heartbeat, Fiona was squatted next to her.

"That was spectacular," she whispered.

"It was just the truth," Sophie whispered back. "I don't want to be her. I just want to be me."

Coach Yates gave a blast on her whistle, and Sophie and Fiona bolted up.

"All right, people," Coach Yates yelled. She yelled everything, but Sophie had discovered that in spite of how mean she looked with her graying ponytail pulled too tight and that evil whistle always at the ready, Coach cared about the kids. She just did it at full volume. Sophie didn't think she deserved her nickname, Coach Hates.

"We're starting a gymnastics unit today!" she hollered. "You'll be in groups of five with one student aide — "

Before the Corn Flakes could even grab onto each other, she added, "Coach Nanini and I have assigned the groups."

"You mean we'll have boys in our group?" Maggie whispered. Sophie thought her Cuban-brown face looked a little pale.

"Group One!" Coach Yates yelled. "Darbie O'Grady. Anne-Stuart Riggins. Sophie LaCroix. Nathan Coffey. And Edward Wornom."

No! *Sophie wanted to yell back at her. How could the coaches do this to her?* They both know Eddie blames me for every scrap of trouble he ever got into! They both know he'll be heinous to me!

Arguing with Coach Yates only got a person after-school detention. Maybe she could talk to Coach Virile.

But Coach Virile was walking toward Group One's mat with his arm around Eddie's shoulders, their heads close as he talked. It didn't look like Coach was warning Eddie. It looked more like he was pumping him up for the Olympics.

Darbie tucked her arm through Sophie's. "This is going to be murder," she said. "I hope the coaches keep their eyes on him."

There aren't enough eyes in this whole school to stop Eddie Wornom, Sophie thought.

Coach Yates was still calling out groups when Darbie and Sophie got to their station. Right in the middle of the Group Six announcement, somebody let out a squeal that echoed through the gym like screeching tires.

It was Julia, literally doing cartwheels toward the Group Six mat, where Jimmy was waiting. Sophie could see the red spots already oozing onto his cheeks.

"I don't think that's because Jimmy's a gymnastics champion," Darbie said.

Willoughby tapped Sophie's shoulder as she ran past her. "Me and Maggie and Fiona are in Group Six too. We'll protect Jimmy for you."

"Student aides are going to teach you the forward roll," Coach Yates yelled, and then gave an extra-long toot on the whistle.

"Who's going to protect us?" Darbie whispered as they hurried toward their mat.

"We just have to keep our power to be ourselves," Sophie said.

Darbie snapped a ponytail holder around her hair and muttered, "Somehow I don't think that's going to be enough."

Sophie tried not to agree with her, even in her mind. No, *she told herself,* we can do this. We have to start with Step One in anti-bullying: ignore him.

A solid-looking eighth-grade girl named Pepper — who had a curved-in waist and thighs bigger than Sophie's hips — demonstrated the forward roll for them and told everybody to try it.

Eddie volunteered to go first.

"Get ready for some eejit thing," Darbie whispered.

Sophie nodded. Eddie did everything the idiot way.

Eddie knelt at the end of the mat, tucked his head under just the way Pepper had told them, and rolled over twice. When he stood up, his gym shorts were down around his hips, revealing a pair of plaid boxers underneath.

"Nobody needs to see that," Darbie whispered.

"Woo-hoo, Eddie!" Anne-Stuart said with the customary sniff.

Eddie hitched up the shorts and said to Pepper, "Sorry. These are from before I lost weight. I'll get new ones."

"You did lose weight," Anne-Stuart purred. She sounded to Sophie like a cat with a sinus problem. "You look good, Eddie."

Eddie shrugged one shoulder and sat down. Sophie and Darbie stared at each other.

He must've learned to be sneakier in military school, Sophie thought. She shivered. This was worse than Eddie just picking her up and trying to stuff her into the garbage. At least back then she had known what she was dealing with.

The Flakes discussed it at lunch.

"Like I said in my email," Fiona told them, "we're going to have to be more vigilant than ever."

"Does vigilant mean 'careful'?" Maggie said.

"It means don't take your eyes off him if he's within a mile of you."

Maggie frowned. "I can't see a whole mile."

"That's why we have to work together," Fiona said. "Report all suspicious Eddie activities to each other, and if we find out something outside of school, we have to email each other."

"I don't have a computer, remember?" Maggie said.

Willoughby slung an arm around her. "That really stinks," she said.

"I feel like I don't know what's going on sometimes."

"I hate that for you," Fiona said.

Darbie put her mini-can of Pringles in front of Maggie. "Don't worry, Mags. We won't let you miss anything."

"Mags can't possibly keep up if she's not online," Fiona told Sophie when they were walking to fifth-period science. "Nobody can. I think I can fix that, though."

Cynthia Cyber nodded at her generous assistant, Dot Com. She was as rich as any of the cyber bullies, but she used her money only for good. If she could get their loyal but computerless staff member online somehow, what strides they could make together in cleaning up the Internet for good. After all, Maga Byte knew all the rules and wasn't afraid to point out when they weren't being followed—

Sophie found herself staring into her science book. Cynthia Cyber was so cool. Maybe there was a way she could fit Dot Com and Maga Byte into the website too.

But that thought was interrupted by Mr. Stires raising his voice. Mr. Stires, their round-faced, bald-headed teacher, was always so cheerful even his toothbrush mustache looked happy. He never spoke above a chuckle.

But right now he was barking. "Why are you using cell phones in my class?"

By the time he stopped in front of Julia and Anne-Stuart, his face was as red as Nathan's. And that was red.

"They're probably text-messaging," Vincent said.

"We are not," Julia said with a roll of her eyes.

Anne-Stuart, of course, sniffed.

"What's text-messaging?" Maggie whispered, but Fiona shook her head.

"May I see, please?" Mr. Stires said.

Anne-Stuart thrust her phone toward him. Julia smiled up, both hands busy with hers under the desktop. Mr. Stires stared at Anne-Stuart's display window amid the somebody's-in-trouble silence in the room.

"This looks like a website," Mr. Stires said.

"It is," Anne-Stuart said. "We were web browsing for our science homework." She delivered a stony stare to Vincent. "And we found one on E. coli."

"Isn't it interesting?" Julia said to Mr. Stires.

"I'm more fascinated by the fact that you can web-browse with your cell phone." Mr. Stires chuckled. "I've read about them, but I haven't seen one yet."

"Look at it all you want," Anne-Stuart said.

Fiona scribbled something on a piece or paper and snapped it onto Sophie's desk.

I'm appalled by what they get away with, it said.

Me too, Sophie wrote back.

Vincent looked openly over their shoulders. "If you had cell phones, you could text-message that to each other. You know that's what they were doing."

Sophie leaned across the aisle toward Jimmy. "We have to put stuff about text-messaging on our website."

"No doubt," he said.

Sophie caught Fiona looking from one of them to the other. Her eyes went flatter and flatter, until they were no more than suspicious dashes. Fiona scribbled on the note paper and thrust it onto Sophie's desk.

It said, I thought you said you didn't LIKE him, like him.

As Sophie crumpled up the note, she wished for the first time ever that she had a cell phone. She could almost see the text message: I DON'T WANT JIMMY FOR A BOYFRIEND!!!!!!!

But watching Fiona slant her gaze over at Jimmy, Sophie wasn't sure even that would do it.

Sophie decided it was a really good thing it was Wednesday and they had Bible

5

study after school. Not only was way-cool Dr. Peter Topping their teacher, but he used to be Sophie's therapist. That meant he could help the Flakes deal with just about any problem by using the Jesus stories.

As the Flakes rode to the church in Fiona's family's big Expedition, with Boppa driving, Sophie tried to decide *which* of her problems to ask Dr. Peter about.

There was Eddie Wornom's coming back to school, acting like he was any normal person, when Sophie knew better. It was like waiting for a snake to strike.

Just as bad in a different way, there was the thing of doing a website instead of a movie. It was turning out to be sort of fun, but not like it would be to *become* Cynthia Cyber and banish a bully from the Internet with fire in her eyes. Or lasers—

But the issue that niggled at her the most was Fiona.

I really want to talk about THAT one at Bible study, Sophie thought. *But how am I going to do it with her sitting right there?*

When they first arrived there was no time to talk about anything, not with so much going on.

Willoughby surprised them by showing up. She hadn't been to Bible study since she'd made cheerleader in September.

"Ms. Hess is only having cheerleading practice twice a week now," she said. "And my dad said he really wanted me to come back to this."

She gave Dr. Peter a shiny smile. Sophie knew Dr. P was working with Willoughby and her dad on some family stuff, which, as far as Sophie was concerned, meant everything was going to be just fine.

Kitty was there too. Since the Flakes didn't get to see her every day, there was a lot of hugging that had to be done. Dr. Peter made sure frail Kitty with her chemotherapy-puffed face was settled in the pink beanbag chair before all of that started. She got to come to Bible study only if she was feeling not-too-awful, and Dr. Peter liked to keep her that way.

He is the best, the best, the best, Sophie thought as she watched him wrinkle his nose to scoot his glasses up and twinkle his blue eyes at the hugging.

When Gill and Harley arrived, he high-fived both of them and plunked Harley's Redskins cap on top of his short, gelled-stiff curls to see how Sophie thought he looked in it.

He always knows what to do for every person, she thought. That decided it. She would talk to him about Fiona after class.

As soon as they all were in their every-one-a-different-color bean-bags, Fiona's hand shot up. Sophie froze. Fiona was *not* going to bring up Jimmy, was she?

"Shoot, Fiona," Dr. Peter said. He rubbed his hands together like somebody was about to give him a big, juicy cheeseburger.

"I have several issues, actually." Fiona looked at Sophie. "But let's start with this one: Eddie Wornom is back." Fiona held up her palms. "Need I say more?"

Sophie let out all her air.

"Up to his old tricks, is he?" Dr. Peter said.

"That's the problem," Darbie said. "He's acting the perfect gentleman." She nodded at the girls, who all nodded with her.

"He's definitely up to something," Fiona said.

"Being a gentleman." Dr. Peter's eyes looked like they were going to twinkle right through his glasses. "That's pretty low."

"It's just an act," Maggie said.

Dr. Peter raised his eyebrows. "And we know this because —"

"Because he isn't capable of being anything but heinous," Fiona said. "He's proved it, like, a million times."

Willoughby gave half a poodle yelp. Kitty whimpered. Harley grunted.

"Looks like we're all in agreement on that," Dr. Peter said. "And I think I have just the story to help us sort this out."

Sophie snatched up the Bible from the floor next to her seat, the one with the purple cover to match her beanbag. She loved this part, where Dr. Peter asked them to imagine they were somebody in the story while he read it out loud.

"Matthew chapter 18," he said. "We'll start at verse 23."

"Who do we have to be?" Maggie said.

"Not somebody evil, I hope," Sophie said. "I don't like it when we have to be the Pharisees."

"Those blackguards," Darbie said.

Dr. Peter grinned. "I wish you girls wouldn't hold back on expressing how you feel. No Pharisees this time. I want you to imagine that you are the forgiven servant."

Sophie closed her eyes and immediately pictured herself in a butler's uniform like she'd seen in a movie once, with a black bow tie and tails on her jacket. She knew they didn't wear those in Bible times, but Dr. Peter always said to go with the visual that made the story clear. Servants in Sophie's World were butlers with towels over their arms, always bowing and saying, "As you wish, sir."

Dr. Peter cleared his throat and read. "'The kingdom of heaven is like a king who wanted to settle accounts with his servants.'"

"You mean, like bank accounts?" Gill said.

"More like loan accounts," Dr. Peter said. "The master's servants often borrowed money from him, and it was time for them to pay him back."

"Okay. Go on," Gill said.

"'As he began the settlement,'" Dr. Peter read, "'a man who owed him ten thousand talents was brought to him.'"

"How much is that?" Maggie said.

A lot, Sophie thought. Can we get on with the story?

"Between fifteen and twenty million dollars," Dr. Peter said. Gill whistled.

"'Since he was not able to pay —'"

"You think?" Willoughby did the poodle thing. "Where's a servant going to get millions of dollars?"

"Exactly," Dr. Peter said. "Shall we go further?"

Please! Sophie thought. It was hard to keep Jenkins the Butler in view with all these interruptions.

"'Since he was not able to pay, the master ordered that he and his wife and his children and all that he had be sold to repay the debt.'"

Jenkins/Sophie fell frozen to the floor. Sell his family—his babies? He buried his face in his hands. He would rather die than be separated from them.

"'The servant'—that's you, ladies—'fell on his knees before him. "Be patient with me," he begged, "and I will pay back everything."'"

Then Jenkins/Sophie flattened himself on the rug before the master, barely daring to breathe unless the master told him to. After all, his whole life was in this powerful man's hands—and not just HIS life.

"'The servant's master took pity on him,'" Dr. Peter read on, "'canceled the debt and let him go.'"

Jenkins/Sophie could hardly believe what he'd heard. He stayed facedown, gasping for air and breathing in rug fibers. Choking and shaking, he pulled himself back up to his knees and clasped his hands over the front of his starched white shirt, now stained with tears. "Thank you, sir," he cried. "Thank you—thank you—thank you."

"'But when that servant went out, he found one of his fellow servants who owed him a hundred denarii.'"

Maggie said, "How much—"

"Just a few dollars," Dr. Peter said. "About a day's wages for a servant. 'He'—well, you, the servant—'grabbed him and began to choke him. "Pay back what you owe me!" he demanded. His fellow servant fell to his knees and begged him, "Be patient with me, and I will pay you back." But he refused. Instead, he went off and had the man thrown into prison until he could pay the debt.'"

Sophie's eyes flew open. "I don't want to imagine myself doing that!" she said. "That's heinous!"

"You aren't the only one who thinks so," Dr. Peter said. "Let's read on."

"I hope this guy's lips get ripped off or something," Gill muttered.

"'When the other servants saw what had happened, they were greatly distressed and went and told their master everything that had happened.'"

"That's what I'm talkin' about," Willoughby said.

"'Then the master called the servant in.'" Dr. Peter paused.

Jenkins/Sophie felt his stomach tighten. Had the master changed his mind? Or was he going to congratulate him for sticking to the rules about people owing you money? Straightening his bow tie, Jenkins/Sophie marched up to the master and said, "How can I help you, sir?"

"'You wicked servant!'" Dr Peter's voice gave Sophie — and Jenkins — a jolt.

Jenkins/Sophie lowered his head and stared at the very rug where only a few hours ago he had felt so relieved, so free.

"'I canceled all that debt of yours because you begged me to. Shouldn't you have had mercy on your fellow servant just as I had on you?' In anger his master turned him over to the jailers.'"

Jenkins/Sophie felt a shock go through him. He couldn't even move his lips to beg. Besides, he knew it would do no good.

"He got what he deserved," Maggie said.

"Did he go to prison for the rest of his life?" Kitty said. Her voice was quivery. She got into the Bible stories almost as much as Sophie did.

"He would be a slave for six years, he and his family," Dr. Peter said. "Not fun."

"So this story means don't borrow money and get in debt," Fiona said. "Like, with credit cards and stuff."

"What if we substitute the word sin for the word debt?" Dr. Peter said. "How does that work in verse 32?"

Sophie followed it on the Bible page with her finger.

"'I canceled all that [sin] of yours because you begged me to,'" Darbie read out loud. "'Shouldn't you have had mercy on your fellow servant just as I had on you?'"

"Now," Dr. Peter said, rubbing his hands together again, "if we put 'God' in place of 'he,' the master, what does the story mean?"

Sophie read it to herself. *"You wicked servant," [God] said. "I canceled all that [sin] of yours because you begged me to. Shouldn't you have had mercy on your fellow servant just as I, [God], had on you?"*

Something pinged in her head.

"You get it, don't you, Sophie-Lophie-Loodle?" Dr. Peter said.

"God forgives us for our sins," Sophie said, "so we should forgive other people for theirs."

"A round of applause for Loodle!"

"I totally get that," Fiona said when they were finished clapping. "What I don't get is what that has to do with Eddie Wornom. No offense or anything."

"None taken." Dr. Peter leaned forward in his beanbag, forearms dangling over his knees. "Looks like we need to watch our Eddie and see how it fits."

"Just once, Dr. Peter," Darbie said, "couldn't you just tell us the answer?"

"No, but I'll help you figure it out."

They all groaned.

"What did the master do to the servant in the end?"

"Threw him in the slammer," Gill said.

"Right, to pay off his debts. So, he wasn't forgiven his debt anymore. What does that say about God's forgiveness?"

Sophie raised her hand. "That we don't get it unless we forgive other people the way he does."

Dr. Peter looked at the rest of the group. "Is she good, or is she good?"

"She's the best," Kitty said.

"Now let me ask you this." Dr. Peter scooted forward some more. "Do you think the servant could ever have paid his master back if the master hadn't forgiven him?"

"Twenty million dollars? On a servant's salary?" Fiona snorted. "No way."

Sophie was sure Fiona was the only one in the room who would know about servants' salaries. The Buntings had a nanny and a cook and a gardener at their house.

"So if we're talking about sins and God, you have to figure only God can dig us out of some of the sin-holes we get ourselves into," Dr. Peter said. "So what two things do we have to do that we've learned from the servant?"

There was a thinking silence.

"He went to the master and begged him," Darbie said.

"Okay — so Number One, we go to God and ask him to forgive us for our sins. And then, Number Two — "

"We gotta forgive other people." Maggie was writing it down in a notebook.

Fiona raised her hand. "What I don't get is why the servant was so evil to the guy that owed him. You'd have thought he would be so happy he'd be in a generous mood." She grinned. "I always ask my dad for stuff when he's just landed a big client or something."

"He was evil," Dr. Peter said, "because he didn't learn anything from being forgiven. The master gave him forgiveness, but he didn't really receive it. Really understanding that you've been forgiven changes something in you."

"Oh," Gill said.

Dr. Peter smacked the sides of his beanbag. "Okay, that's a lot to think about. Let me give you your assignment and then we'll eat."

"Ready," Maggie said, pen poised over the notebook.

"Every day between now and next Wednesday, I want you to confess your sins to God in your quiet time. Think of the things you did or didn't do that probably disappointed God. Be really specific. Lay them all out for him, and ask him to cancel those things out in his mind as if they never happened, because you can never make up for all that stuff. See if it doesn't make you feel like you're starting over with a clean record after you do it."

"I get it!" Willoughby said with a mini-yelp. "Like the beginning of every report-card period—you don't have any tardies or anything."

"Only you can do this as many times a day as you want." Dr. Peter twinkled a smile.

"Did you say there was food?" Gill said.

"How 'bout hot chocolate and Christmas cookies?" he said. "I want to get you in the right mood."

The door came open and Kitty's mom, Mrs. Munford, backed in and pivoted around with a tray of steaming mugs with snowmen on them. Darbie's aunt Emily followed with two plates heaped with red-and-green-sprinkled cookies. Sophie felt a pang of missing Mama. She would have so been here with her double-fudge brownies if she could.

"So what are we getting in the right mood for?" Fiona said when they were all circled around the cookie piles, mugs in hand.

"For a project I hope you'll do," Dr. Peter said. "It's mostly for you filmmakers, but Gill, you and Harley can be involved if you want."

The Wheaties exchanged glances and shook their heads. "We're not actors," Gill said.

"You want us to make a movie?" Sophie rose to her knees. "That would be — "

"Fabulous!" Fiona said.

"You haven't even heard what it is yet," Dr. Peter said. "I'm thinking we need a movie for the little kids at church on the true meaning of Christmas. Something they can really get. I know it's short notice, with Christmas just three weeks away."

"Leave it to us, Dr. P," Darbie said. "Sophie will dream up characters, and we'll work out a script — "

"I already have the script." Dr. Peter reached behind his bean-bag and pulled up a folder.

"We don't do it that way," Maggie said.

"But we could." Sophie gave Dr. Peter an extra-big smile in case his feelings were hurt. "What's it about?"

"You know ''Twas the Night Before Christmas'?" he said. "It's like that, but it's about Jesus instead of Santa. It could probably use some doctoring up."

"Sounds ... fascinating," Sophie said. Fiona was already midway through a not-so-tactful eye roll.

"The only problem is that it requires some male types."

"We have boys," Sophie said. "I mean, not boyfriends — you know, just boys we do movies with."

"You know Jimmy will help." Darbie nudged Sophie with her elbow. Willoughby collapsed against Maggie. Dr. Peter looked bewildered.

"Okay, then, so I take it you're up for it?" he said.

"We'll make it amazing," Fiona said. "With or without boys."

Darbie nodded. "We're in."

Sophie was too jazzed to even speak. Yes! A chance for Cynthia to make a film after all. Surely there would be a spot for her —

Dr. Peter passed out enough scripts for each of them and the Lucky Charms, in case they agreed to help. But when they climbed into the Expedition with Boppa and read the script, Sophie wasn't so sure they would.

In the first place, there was obviously no room in the script for Cynthia Cyber.

But that wasn't the only problem.

"Is it just me," Fiona said, "or is this the corniest thing you've ever read?"

"It's absolutely cheesy," Darbie said.

Maggie looked up soberly. "You and Fiona write way better than this, Sophie."

"No doubt," Fiona said.

"We can't hurt Dr. Peter's feelings, though," Sophie said.

"Let's just change some of the lines so they don't sound like Miss Odetta would say them." Fiona leaned forward and rubbed the back of Boppa's bald head. "No offense, Boppa."

Miss Odetta used to be Fiona and her brother and sister's nanny. Now she was married to Boppa, and she was so old-fashioned, she gave Fiona demerits when she didn't act like a lady.

"I take it you don't want it to sound completely proper," Boppa said.

Boppa's caterpillar eyebrows filled the rearview mirror, but Sophie knew his eyes were smiling.

"There's sounding proper and then there's sounding like a grammar book," Fiona said. "Those little kids will be climbing up the walls after the first five minutes."

Darbie suddenly let out a giggle, which didn't happen often. "One thing works," she said. "There's a married couple in it. Sophie and Jimmy can play them."

"What?" Sophie grabbed the script from Darbie.

"Should I write that down?" Maggie said.

Sophie's voice squeaked up into the only-dogs-can-hear range. "We don't even know if the Lucky Charms will do this with us yet."

"Do we really need them?" Fiona said. "We used to play the boy roles all the time before."

"No offense, Fiona," Darbie said. "But I think we're too old for that now. Besides"—her eyes sparkled—"Sophie and Jimmy would be—"

"Okay, okay." Fiona swatted her hands like she was beating down a bee swarm. "We'll ask them."

"We should have a meeting," Maggie said. She still had her pen ready.

"My house?" Darbie said.

"No," Fiona said. "We'll meet on the Internet tonight at seven. Go to our website. You'll see a private chat room I just set up for us. Well, my dad did. Anyway, I'll call Vincent, and he can call Nathan. Darb, you let Kitty and Willoughby know."

Darbie smiled slyly at Sophie. "You call Jimmy, Soph," she said. "No!"

"I can't meet in a chat room," Maggie said. Her voice was as matter-of-fact as always, but Sophie could see a left-out look in her eyes.

"Aw, Mags, we forgot again," Darbie said.

"Come home with me now, Mags," Fiona said. "Boppa can call your mom. Besides, I want us to talk to my dad about something."

"You actually have a chat room for us?" Darbie said.

Fiona nodded. "I can be very useful when it comes to websites." She slit her eyes at Sophie. They had completely lost their magic. "I *know* I'm better at it than Jimmy Wythe," she added.

Sophie felt stung. Fiona was suddenly looking a lot like a Corn Pop, and it made her shiver.

I didn't get to talk to Dr. Peter about it, either, she thought.

But it looked like she'd better. And soon.

The Flakes and the Charms all gathered in the chat room that night. It was Sophie's first time chatting, but once she figured out it was just like IM'ing, only with a bunch of people, she caught on right away.

It was a good thing it didn't matter who said what because it was hard to keep the screen names straight. Besides Darbie's IRISH and Fiona's WORDGRL and Kitty's MEOW and Jimmy's Go4Gold, there was Willoughby as CHEER and Nathan as SWASH. That was short for Swashbuckler, since he was all into swordplay. Vincent was COMPTRGEEK. He was the only person Sophie knew who was proud to be a geek. *That's taking the power to be yourself to a whole new level*, she thought.

By eight o'clock, plans for Dr. Peter's Christmas movie were a done deal. The parts were doled out, with Jimmy and Sophie as the husband and wife by popular vote. Except for Fiona, who pointed out that Vincent should be the husband since he actually looked older than Jimmy. Vincent almost freaked out right on the screen. He liked to stay behind the camera. After that, Sophie could feel Fiona pouting out there in cyberspace.

It wasn't MY idea, Fiona, Sophie wanted to type in.

But at least it wasn't some creepy Fruit Loop. She thought it might not be *too* evil with Jimmy. Fiona shooting eye darts at her was a worse image.

The rehearsal schedule fell into place, and Maggie was ready to research pictures of costumes for her mom, Senora LaQuita, to make. That led to some discussion.

COMPTRGEEK:	*How's Mag going to do that when she doesn't have a computer?*
WORDGRL:	*She does now.*
CHEER:	*you bought her one?*
MEOW:	*I knew you were rich Fiona but WOW!!!!!!!!!!!!*
WORDGRL:	*My dad gave her one of our old ones. Boppa's setting it up at her house tomorrow.*
IRISH:	*Boppa?*
WORDGRL:	*I found out he knows all about computers. Who knew?*
DREAMGRL:	*He got hip.*
SWASH:	*Huh?*
MEOW:	*POS Gotta go!!!!!!!!!!*
CHEER:	*BYE everybuddy.*

Sophie smiled at her screen. The Internet was like having everyone there with her any time she wanted. And now even Maggie got to do it.

Fiona's being pretty rude to me right now, Sophie thought, *but she really is good inside.*

Sophie just wished she would be "good" about the Round Table website. And Jimmy.

I'm gonna write her an email, Sophie thought.

She had just clicked out of the chat room when the happy little bell told her she had an IM.

ANGELEYES: Hi Sofee

Who's that? Sophie thought. She knew from the conference not to respond to people she didn't know.

ANGELEYES: It's me Anne-Stuart.

Sophie stared. Anne-Stuart was IM'ing *her*? And her screen name was *Angel Eyes*? *Oh, brother.*

She must be up to something, Sophie thought. Carefully Sophie typed and then clicked Send.

DREAMGRL: Hi

ANGELEYES: *I'm sorry Julia said you couldn't get a boyfriend. That was kinda mean. Don't tell her I said that, k?*

Before Sophie could even think how to answer, the bell dinged again.

ANGELEYES: *Well — bye*

DREAMGRL: *Bye. Thanks*

Something pinged, like the IM bell going off in her mind.

She did apologize. I'm supposed to forgive her.

Which reminded her —

Sophie crawled through the chiffon curtains and onto her bed, where she closed her eyes. Dr. Peter had said to confess every day.

It wasn't hard for Sophie to talk to Jesus. Dr. Peter had taught her to imagine him and tell him everything. She never imagined him answering because that would be like writing his lines for him. But she could always "see" his kind eyes, and there was always an answer sometime, somewhere, if she watched for it.

Jesus, she thought to him, *it's a good thing you have time for everybody because I'm going to confess all my sins to you, and that could take a while.*

She started off with the first sin she could remember, which was when she was four and she didn't come when Mama called her for lunch because she was busy pretending she was Sleeping Beauty, and she was right in the middle of the sleeping part.

By the time she got through with the sins of year four, Sophie decided she'd better stick with just the ones from that day.

So, Jesus, she prayed, *I'm really sorry I didn't help Lacie clean up the kitchen this morning because I went to school early.*

And I think it hurt Fiona's feelings when I was working with Jimmy on the website and didn't invite her. Only I didn't do that on purpose. I didn't know she would care—only I should have known because she always gets funky if she thinks I might get a different best friend. Like I would be best friends with a boy! But I'm sorry I forgot that about her.

Sophie scrunched her eyes shut tighter. So far, none of her sins seemed so bad. She was going to have to look harder.

I think I'm sorry that we played that trick on the Pops. I just wanted them to feel lame the way they're always making us feel. Only that's against our Code, and since you, like, wrote the Code for us, I guess I'm in trouble with you. Will you please forgive me?

But Jesus, don't you have to admit we really got them good?

Sophie sank back against the pillows with a sigh. This was harder than she'd expected it to be.

Wow, she thought. *It must take some people the whole night to confess.*

Some people, like Eddie Wornom.

Sophie scrunched her eyes again. She was pretty sure she better get forgiveness for that thought.

When Sophie got on the bus the next morning and sat behind the Wheaties, they both turned around and stared at her.

"What?" Sophie wiped at her nose. "Do I have a booger hanging out or something?"

"No," Gill said. "We just don't get why you'd want a boyfriend. Boys are lame."

"I don't want one," Sophie said.

"That's not what I heard. I heard you and Jimmy Gymnast were going out."

"Heard from who?" Sophie said.

Gill twisted her mouth. "See, that's the thing. I don't exactly know."

"How could you not know who told you?" Sophie put up her hand. "Forget it. Just so you know, Jimmy Wythe and I are not going out."

"We didn't think you'd do something stupid like that," Gill said. "That's why we asked you."

But no one else Sophie saw that day bothered to ask. All she heard from the time she stepped off the bus were things like —

"So you and that gymnastics dude are going out."

"Congratulations, Sophie. He's cute."

Half those people Sophie didn't even know. By the time she got to third period, she'd received five notes from girls who had never noticed she was alive before, not to mention a slew of comments from faceless voices in the hall saying everything from "Poor Jimmy" to "Ya'll make the cutest couple!"

Almost the only person who didn't say anything to her was Jimmy himself. He spent all of first-and-second-period block behind his literature book with about six red blotches on each cheek.

So when someone behind her in the gym locker hall said, "Why am I the last person to know Little Bit loves Jimbo?" she would have decked him if he hadn't been Coach Virile.

He grinned down at her, and Sophie gave him her most dramatic sigh.

"Is there anybody in this whole school who isn't talking about it?" Sophie said.

"Nope. It's the main topic of conversation."

Sophie put her hands on her hips. "Can I make an announcement on the intercom that Jimmy and I are not going out? Can't a girl and a boy just be friends?"

"Around here? Evidently not," Coach Virile said. "So it's only a rumor, huh?"

"Yes!"

He bent over and put his hands on his knees so he was closer to Sophie's level. "I'm actually glad to hear that because I think middle school is way too early for" — he made quotation marks with his fingers — 'relationships.' There will be plenty of time for boyfriends when you're older, Little Bit."

"That's what I keep saying, but nobody believes me!"

"It'll die down, just as soon as they find something else to gossip about." Coach Virile gave her another grin. "Doesn't anybody talk about football anymore?"

I HOPE it dies down, Sophie thought as she pushed her way through the girls' locker room. *And the sooner the better.*

But that didn't look promising when she arrived at her locker. Two girls were standing in front of it, and they practically pounced on her.

"So *you're* Sophie," one of them said.

The other one smacked the girl on the arm. "I told you it was her."

"Wow," said Girl #1 to Sophie. "I thought you'd be cuter."

"No offense," said Girl #2.

"I need to open my locker," Sophie said.

"Oh, sorry," said Girl #1. She grabbed Girl #2's hand and they went off whispering.

Sophie turned to the Flakes, who were already half dressed.

"What's going on?" she said.

"Simple." Maggie jerked her head toward B.J. and Cassie, who were hissing to Julia and Anne-Stuart.

"They talked about you guys going out all first and second periods," Willoughby said.

"But it isn't true!" Sophie said.

Darbie took Sophie's discarded clothes and shoved them into her locker for her. "We made them think it was, remember?"

"Only they've embellished it," Fiona said.

"Does that mean they exaggerated?" Maggie said.

"More like they decorated what we said with lies." Fiona's voice tightened. "Or are they?"

"Some eejit told me you'd been dating in secret since last year," Darbie said. "And we know that's a lie."

Willoughby looked wide-eyed at Sophie. "It *is* a lie, right?"

"Hel-*lo*!" Sophie looked at Fiona, who didn't look back.

"Sorry," Willoughby said.

Sophie plunked herself down on the bench to put on her shoes. "I hope Jimmy doesn't think I'm telling everybody all this stuff."

"Maybe you should ask him," Maggie said.

"You want me to ask him for you?" Willoughby said.

"I can do it," Sophie said.

"Let Willoughby do it," Fiona said.

But sending somebody else sounded to Sophie too much like something one of the Pops would do if she actually liked a guy. They always made everything so complicated with boys.

Still, Sophie's mouth went dry as she headed for Jimmy in the gym. But before she could get to him, he came to her. His red spots had been reduced to two, and he was smiling.

"Pretty funny, huh?" he said. "All the stuff they're saying about us."

"Funny?" Sophie looked at him closely. "You aren't mad about it, are you? Because I didn't start it—"

"What's to get mad about? I'm laughing all over the place."

"Oh," Sophie said. He was right, of course. Du-uh—that's what you did with bullies.

He bent his blond head toward her and lowered his voice. "Did you know we were getting married?"

"What?"

"Planning the wedding and everything. I mean, come on— who's gonna believe that?"

He had the most perfect are-these-people-lame-or-what expression on his face, Sophie spit out a laugh. Jimmy grinned and pretended to wipe her saliva off his shirt.

"All right, lovebirds, break it up!" Coach Yates yelled.

"See you at the wedding," Jimmy whispered to Sophie.

"Do we have to invite *her*?" Sophie whispered back.

Jimmy's words nudged at Sophie like mischievous elves. So when Pepper asked her

7

if she wanted her to try to get Jimmy switched with Nathan so they could be in the same gymnastics group, Sophie just laughed out loud. Now, if Pepper had asked her to switch *Eddie* with Jimmy, that would have been a different matter.

Eddie *did* do his forward rolls and his tripods and his headstands like Pepper told him to. But Sophie wasn't fooled. After all, he was still hanging with Tod and Colton outside classes. And she'd seen Eddie come out of Coach Virile's office about five times.

He isn't fooling Coach Virile, either, Sophie thought. She launched into her forward roll—and couldn't stop rolling. When she did, she was in the middle of the gym.

Before she could even get up, Eddie was there, sticking his hand down to her.

"Want help?" he said.

Somewhere in the direction of Group Four, Sophie heard Colton clapping like an ape.

"I'm *fine*." Sophie scrambled up by herself. *How stupid do you think I am?* she wanted to ask. Yeah, she still needed to watch Eddie — along with the thousand other things she had to do.

She and Jimmy met Thursday and Friday mornings before school to write their website proposal for Round Table. Both days Fiona shot her so many pointy looks during first period, Sophie felt like she needed Band-Aids.

I know she gets all possessive, Sophie thought, *but for Pete's sake, I'm spending all the rest of my time with her!*

Thursday and Friday at lunch and after school, and all day Saturday, the Flakes and Charms worked on their Dr. Peter Christmas movie. Most of that time they were rewriting the script. The whole thing. There didn't seem to be a line in the original that didn't make everyone's eyes roll. A couple of times Sophie thought Fiona's might disappear up into her head.

"'It is the wee hours of the morning, sir,'" Fiona read in a fakey-deep voice Saturday afternoon. "'What business have you with us?'" She looked at the group with her mouth open. "Nobody talks like that."

"It's set in the Victorian era," Vincent said.

"I bet they didn't talk like that then, either," Fiona said stubbornly.

"So what do you want it to say?" Maggie tapped her gel pen on the open Treasure Book.

Jimmy let an easy smile spread across his face. "How 'bout 'Yo, dude, what's up? It's three o'clock in the morning.'"

"Yeah," Sophie said. "'Whatta you want'?"

Jimmy laughed. "'It better be good because when somebody wakes me up, man, it can get ugly.'"

"You know it," Sophie said, giggling.

"Do I write that down?" Maggie said.

"Yeah, that's good!" Nathan said.

Fiona knotted her lips. "I don't know, Jimmy. It's pretty lame."

Jimmy blinked. Sophie glared at Fiona.

"It isn't lame, it's a gas," Darbie said.

"It won't go with Victorian costumes then," Fiona said.

Sophie was immediately serious. "Don't change the costumes!" She'd already fallen in love with the gown Senora LaQuita was making for her. It even had a corset underneath that made her stand up very straight.

"You know what would be mega-funny?" Vincent said. His big, loose grin took up half his face. "If we did everything Victorian, even, like, with those proper voices, but we used modern language, like you guys just did."

"That would be class!" Darbie said.

"It isn't supposed to be funny." Maggie tapped harder with the gel pen.

"Why not?" Vincent said. "The kids'll laugh, but they'll still get the point."

"Yeah! Kind of like a Disney movie," Willoughby said, "where it's all slapstick, and then you have a serious part where you end up crying."

"Yeah," Jimmy said. He tilted his head at Sophie. "You're not saying anything."

Eyes half closed, Sophie nodded slowly.

"Uh-oh, she's dreaming," Fiona said. "I know that look."

"But is she dreaming the same thing we're dreaming?" Vincent said.

Sophie blinked at him. "That depends."

"On what?" Darbie said.

"On whether I can be called Louisa Linkhart and act *way* proper."

"Oh, yeah, we can't use Cynthia Cyber, huh," Jimmy said.

Fiona's face went stiff. "Who's Cynthia Cyber?"

"Internet Investigator," Jimmy said. "She's for the website."

Fiona rolled her eyes *and* her head. "Come *on*, Jimmy," she said. "You can't have some Internet chick in a Victorian movie. That *is* lame."

Jimmy turned even redder than Nathan.

"He knows that," Sophie said through clenched teeth. "He just said that."

"Okay!" Vincent said. "I vote we let Sophie be this Louey Linkey chick and act as proper as she wants. That'll make it really funny when she says, like — "

"'You get your tail out of here unless you have a death wish,'" Sophie/Louisa said. She made every letter distinct.

"I love that!" Willoughby cried.

Everyone joined in with their individual versions of Willoughby's poodle yelp. That was, everyone except Fiona, who slit her eyes like a full-fledged Corn Pop.

It got worse on the way to Fiona's after rehearsal. Sophie was going to spend the night, but all Fiona did on the ride was concentrate on her cuticles.

This is gonna get ugly, Sophie thought.

They were barely in Fiona's room when Fiona dropped her backpack on the floor and, hands on hips, ripped out with, "How come you didn't tell *me* about Cynthia Cyber?"

Sophie sank down on the bed and counted the leopard spots on the pillowcase trim before she answered. It was better to think things through, she knew, when it came to a word-fight with Fiona.

"I didn't tell you because you're not working on the website," Sophie said finally.

"Yet," Fiona said. She sat heavily next to Sophie. "You're asking Round Table if we can all help, right?"

Sophie hadn't actually considered that, but she nodded. She could feel Fiona's eye darts going right through her.

"Sure," she said. "I mean, if it's okay with Jimmy."

"Is he the boss of you now?" Fiona said.

Sophie grabbed the pillow and smacked her with it.

Fiona grabbed it and smashed it down beside her. "Don't change the subject," she said.

"What subject?" Sophie said.

"And don't try to stall me, either. I want to know if you have to check everything out with Jimmy now. It sure seems like it."

Fiona's eyes narrowed as she punched her fist down into the pillow. Sophie felt like it was her stomach that had taken the hit.

"No," Sophie said. "But we're both doing the website. It wouldn't be right for me to just say we're gonna do something when he has half the say." She gnawed at her lip. "I can't be rude to him like you're being."

"I'm just being honest." Fiona glared at the pillow. "And I wasn't just talking about the website."

"Then *what*?"

"I'm hungry." Fiona headed for the door like she was starving. But Sophie knew she wasn't.

It's a hard enough job Internet investigating, Cynthia Cyber thought as she followed Dot Com to the kitchen. *Why does she have to make it even MORE complicated?*

Fiona didn't have much to say the rest of the weekend. Sophie chewed on that until Monday. Finishing the website proposal with Jimmy that day helped. When they took it to Round Table at lunch, Hannah didn't give them twenty-five reasons why it wouldn't work. Oliver only snapped his rubber bands once, and that was when Sophie mentioned involving people outside of Round Table.

"I think it should just be the people who went to the conference," he said.

"Feeling exclusive, are you, Oliver?" Miss Imes said, her eyebrows pointing up as sharply as her voice.

"No," Oliver said. "But if this is such a big deal and people could get really wrecked by the whole cyber-bullying thing, it should be done by the people that know what it's all about."

Miss Imes nodded her head of crisp, almost-white hair. "Excellent reason. I underestimated you."

The rest of the group gave Oliver polite applause, while Sophie chewed at her bottom lip again. Fiona wasn't going to like this. At all.

Fiona *didn't* like it. Even after Sophie explained to her at least twelve times that it was a Round Table decision, Fiona still drilled her eyes into Sophie. "They're the ones who are losing out, then," she said.

She opened her mouth as if she were going to say more, and then she snapped it shut.

"*What?*" Sophie said. "If you're thinking Jimmy's my new best friend or something, we have *so* been through this before — first Maggie, then Darbie."

Fiona rolled her eyes. "That was back when I was immature," she said. "Just forget it, okay? And tell those Round Table people I could help you build an awesome website."

Then she knotted her mouth, and Sophie knew the conversation was over. *Besides*, Sophie thought, *the Round Table website is already amazing*.

They had Jimmy's quiz, and sample situations of cyber bullying where web visitors could click on what they thought were the best solutions. When her picture popped up, Cynthia Cyber would then tell them if they were right or wrong. The drawing that Mrs. Britt chose to represent Cynthia Cyber wasn't exactly how Sophie imagined her, but at least she was there.

Sophie tried to get Dot Com and Maga Byte in there too, but she and Jimmy decided that would make it too confusing. They already had so much information to include to help kids who were being bullied. They settled on a list of basics with little graphics of computers to click on for more information.

1. WHEN YOU'RE CYBER-BULLIED FOR THE FIRST TIME, DON'T RESPOND. THAT WILL ONLY MAKE THE SITUATON WORSE. MOST BULLIES GO AWAY IF YOU IGNORE THEM.

2. IF YOU'RE BULLIED AGAIN, PRINT OUT THE BULLYING MATERIAL AND SAVE IT IN CASE YOU NEED EVIDENCE. BLOCK ALL EMAILS FROM THE SENDER. THE HELP MENU ON YOUR EMAIL PRO-GRAM WILL SHOW YOU HOW.

3. IF THE BULLYNG KEEPS UP AND YOU FIND OUT WHO'S DOING IT, TELL YOUR PARENTS OR ANOTHER ADULT. ASK THEM TO CALL THE BULLY'S PARENTS.

4. IF THAT DOESN'T WORK, REPORT THE HARASSMENT TO SCHOOL OFFICIALS AND SEND YOUR EVIDENCE TO THE BULLY'S INTERNET SERVICE PROVIDER.

5. IF A CYBER BULLY THREATENS YOU WITH PHYSI-CAL HARM, TELL YOUR PARENTS AND ASK THEM TO CALL THE POLICE. *CYBER STALKING IS A CRIME!*

On another webpage they had everything about how to prevent Internet bullying. They included things like "netiquette" — manners online. And how to have a strong code of personal behavior so you don't bully, even though no one may ever catch you.

One of the best parts of the website, Sophie thought, *was the "Acceptable Use Policy" that everyone in the school would have to sign before they could use school computers.* That seemed so wonderfully official to Sophie, and she and Jimmy always referred to it as the AUP. They didn't come up with the idea themselves — a lot of schools were doing it — but Cynthia Cyber heartily approved.

Working on the website could have occupied all of Sophie's time, if she hadn't also been working on the movie and helping at home, plus chatting, emailing, and IM'ing on the computer. Her Internet time got cut back, though, when Lacie complained that she could never get online to do her homework. Daddy limited Sophie to an hour a day. It was like losing a finger or something.

And then there was school. It was getting hard to keep up, but Sophie knew she had to maintain at least a B in everything to keep her camera. Actually, school wouldn't have been so bad if she hadn't ended up with Anne-Stuart every time a teacher assigned a group activity. *What happened to us making our own groups?* Sophie wondered more than once. Anne-Stuart was never openly snotty to her — especially not in language arts/social studies block where they had both Mrs. Clayton and Ms. Hess patrolling the classroom. But the too-nice approach she was using made Sophie feel like she needed Pepto-Bismol. Sophie thought she must be getting tips from that snake Eddie Wornom.

"Doesn't it bother you that Julia is always in groups with Jimmy?" Anne-Stuart said to Sophie one day in Miss Imes' class when their group was figuring out story problems.

Sophie glanced at the group in the corner. Julia had her desk touching Jimmy's and appeared to be writing something on his paper. When she saw Sophie looking, she smiled a plastic smile and waved.

"She's totally flirting with your guy," Anne-Stuart said.

It did no good to protest for the ninety-fifth time that Jimmy wasn't her "guy."

Another day, Anne-Stuart showed up first period with an elastic bandage wrapped around her right wrist, saying she'd hurt it in PE the day before. She asked Sophie, in a cotton-candy voice, if she would email the group's notes to her that night since she couldn't write. The bandage disappeared by third period, and, come to think of it, Sophie didn't remember seeing Anne-Stuart hurt it in the first place.

But I'll email her the notes anyway. That's what a Corn Flake does, Sophie told herself. Thankfully, there weren't that many notes.

There was definitely a lot going on, but Sophie remembered to confess everything to Jesus at night before she went to sleep.

I'm sorry I keep thinking the Corn Pops are the most heinous people in the galaxy. Even if they are, I shouldn't be thinking that. I just wish they'd stop with the Jimmy thing already. HE'S NOT MY BOYFRIEND.

I gotta confess that I'm getting sick of Fiona pouting about the website. But I guess I would feel kinda hurt if it was me.

I hate it that I wanted to flush Zeke down the toilet today when he used my curtains for a Spider-Man web and tried to swing from the window to the bed. I hope Daddy can fix my curtain rod this weekend.

She always fell asleep before she got through the whole list. She liked getting a fresh start every day, but the teasing about Jimmy started the minute she set foot in the school. When she wished she could shove them all into the nearest garbage can, she knew there would be plenty more to confess that night.

But none of that teasing could compare to what happened Sunday.

When Sophie sat down to check her email after church, there were five messages.

8

Three were from Fiona, which she was almost afraid to read. One was from Jimmy. The fifth one had an address she'd never seen before.

She hesitated with the cursor pointed at the Read icon. The website said not to open mail from unknown senders — but maybe this was just somebody who had never emailed her, like one of the Wheaties.

I'll just look at it, and if it's trash I'll delete it, she decided.

Sofee, the email said. Check out this cool website.

Sophie clicked on the website address. The minute she saw it, she turned to ice.

Who's getting together at gmms?

it said. And before the visitor could even wonder, there was the answer, complete with a photograph of Jimmy and Sophie huddled up like they were peeking out an imaginary window together.

"That was when we were practicing for the movie during lunch Friday!" she said out loud. "It was right out in the courtyard! Who took that?"

Sophie's hand was so cold she could barely scroll down the page.

There was a "quote" from Sophie's own screen name.

DREAMGRL: *I've been after him for a long time. Now he's mine.*

Then came a cut-out photograph of Sophie's head. When Sophie clicked on the icon, there was a recording in her own voice saying, "I'm in love." Her photographed mouth moved like a robot's.

Below that was a picture of Jimmy with his mouth open and a written quote: "I wanted Julia, but she's going out with Colton now. Lucky guy. Sophie's okay, but—"

For More, Click Here, the instructions read. Sophie did, and heard Jimmy's voice saying, "She's got some serious mental problems."

It ended with—

To Follow Jimmy/Sophie, Check This Website Daily. To End, Click Here.

Sophie did and was rewarded with a loud kissing sound.

Even after the images disappeared from the screen, Sophie sat staring at it. *It's not true!* she thought over and over. *It's all made up!*

And then it pinged in her head. She'd just been cyber-bullied.

Okay—okay, she thought. *What am I supposed to do?*

She smacked her forehead with the heel of her hand. *Du-uh. I WROTE the rules!*

No more going to that website. That was Step One. But she was still shivering. She decided to skip a couple of steps and tell Daddy.

It was DOS — "daughter over shoulder" — as Daddy perused *Who's Getting Together* on his computer in the study, making disgusted noises in his throat.

"Isn't Jimmy that kid you're doing the website with?" he said.

"Yes."

"You two aren't — "

"Daddy!"

"I'm just asking. They've got a picture of you both here."

"We were practicing for our movie!"

"And the recording of your voice?"

"I don't know how they got that. We were just messing around in the locker room, playing a joke."

"That's your screen name, isn't it? Dream Girl?"

"But I never wrote that! I don't even think it!"

Daddy put his hand on top of Sophie's head and gently pushed her down to sit beside him. "Okay, Baby Girl, I'm on your side. I'm just showing you how easy it is for people to get images and sound bites and 'prove' anything they want to." He grunted. "These kids should be working for the tabloids."

"What are those?"

"Those newspapers in the grocery store checkout line with the stuff about space aliens and Elvis coming back."

"That's so totally what this is!" Sophie said. "Only how did they get all this stuff? How did somebody get my email address?"

And did Jimmy really say I had some serious mental problems? she added to herself. She was suddenly having a hard time swallowing.

"All right, here's the game plan," Daddy said. "I'm going to move your and Lacie's computers into the family room."

"Why?" Sophie said.

"Why? You gave me the rules — right there in that stuff for parents from the conference. It said to not let your child use a computer in a private place like the bedroom." Daddy grinned at her as he ruffled up her hair. "That will teach you to be such a good kid, huh?" His blue eyes got softer. "Look, I know you feel like you're being punished for what somebody else is doing, but I just think I need to keep a closer eye on what goes on with your computer use. I promise I won't POS you too much."

Sophie's eyes bulged. "I shouldn't have given you that stuff," she said.

Daddy laughed. After he moved the computers into the family room, Lacie glared at Sophie for the rest of the day.

Sophie could barely drag herself into the school on Monday. If *she* had seen the website, the rest of GMMS had probably seen it too.

But nobody mentioned it before school or during the first block. Not even Fiona.

Maybe they really have moved on to the next thing to gossip about, Sophie thought. *Just like Coach Virile said.*

Cynthia Cyber sighed. At last the young people were starting to understand: if cyber bullying got them no attention, they would soon stop. She rubbed her hands together and went for the mouse again. There was still much work to be done —

"There is a rule at this school about cell phones in class." Mrs. Clayton's voice trumpeted across the room.

Sophie turned around to see Tod blinking innocently. He looked like a character from Dr. Seuss, the way everything on his face came to a point at the end of his nose, but he wasn't fooling Sophie. There was a cell phone someplace on his person.

"It's a good rule too, Mrs. C," he said. "How would anybody get any work done if people were sending out pictures to everybody's cell phones?"

Julia smacked him on the back of the head with her binder. Anne-Stuart went into a coughing fit.

"Is that what's going on?" Mrs. Clayton was now on him like an angry goose. Ms. Hess was closing in from behind.

"I don't know." Tod shrugged. "I don't have a cell phone."

"Frisk him, Mrs. C!" said Colton as he grinned at Tod. "Make sure he isn't lyin'."

"Shut *up*!" Tod said.

"*Everyone* be quiet!" Mrs. Clayton's trumpet voice hit a new high. Even Ms. Hess jumped.

"Now," Mrs. Clayton said, "this is your warning: leave your cell phones in your lockers when you come to this class. Any that I find in this room will be confiscated and you can retrieve them from Mr. Bentley."

Mr. Bentley was the principal. You didn't want to have to go to his office.

"What was that whole thing about the cell phones?" Darbie said when the Corn Flakes were on their way to PE.

"Did it happen in your class too?" Maggie said. "Everybody was looking at their phones and laughing." She squared her shoulders. "They're not supposed to have them in class."

Sophie looked at Willoughby, who lagged behind them. "You have a cell phone," she said. "Do you know?"

Willoughby wouldn't look at her.

"You do know," Fiona said. "Come on, dish."

"I don't want to," Willoughby said.

"Why not?" Darbie said.

Willoughby wound a curl around her finger. "Because it's about Sophie."

They all stopped. Sophie felt herself go cold again.

"Was it a text message?" Fiona poked Willoughby. "What did it say about Sophie?"

"It wasn't a text message." Willoughby sounded like every word was painful to say. "It was a picture."

"You can't get pictures on a cell phone," Maggie said flatly.

"You can if it's a camera phone," Fiona said. "Was it of Sophie?"

Willoughby gave a miserable nod. "She was putting on her shorts in the locker room." Her eyes popped at Sophie. "You couldn't really see your underwear or anything."

"I admit that's pretty rude," Fiona said. "But it's not like *that* bad."

"There were words with it, though." Willoughby looked like she was going to throw up. "It said, 'Hey, Jimmy, look who has the ugliest body at GMMS.'"

She threw her arms around Sophie, but Sophie peeled her off. Although her lips were frozen, she managed to say, "We have to tell. It says so on our website."

"Let's see it, Will," Darbie said.

But Willoughby shook her head. There were tears shining in her eyes. "I erased it. I didn't want Sophie to see it."

Sophie sagged. "Then we don't have any evidence."

"And you *know* nobody else around here is going to turn them in," Darbie said. "The blackguards."

Maggie jerked her head toward the locker room. "We're gonna be late."

But as the rest of the Corn Flakes hurried inside, Fiona tugged Sophie to a stop.

"I know the Pops are being mean, Soph," she said. Her eyes looked motherly. "But they wouldn't even be doing it if it didn't look like you and Jimmy were practically engaged."

"It doesn't look like that!"

Fiona wiggled Sophie's sleeve. "Evidently it does to them. I'm just saying, think about it."

It was impossible to think about anything else from then on. Sophie could barely change into her PE clothes for fear there were hidden cameras everywhere. The other Corn Flakes kept close watch on the Pops while she wriggled into her shorts. They were on backward, but she left them that way.

During class she went through the gymnastics moves like an icicle. Anne-Stuart did hers perfectly, which made Sophie wish she had faked a heart attack and gone to the nurse instead. Eddie acted like he was zipped inside a sleeping bag — that was how much attention he paid to anybody. Sophie didn't even try to guess what was going on with him.

In fact, by the time she got to fourth period, Sophie was in such a frozen state she stared for a good two minutes at the paper Miss Imes put on her desk before she realized it was a test. A test she'd forgotten to study for. When they exchanged papers and graded them at the end of class, Sophie's came back to her from Darbie with a D on it and a tiny sad face.

She was ready to cry, especially when Miss Imes stopped her after class. "Sophie, you were doing so well again, and now lately you've slacked off."

"I'll be okay," Sophie said.

"You're distracted." Miss Imes pointed her eyebrows up to her hairline. "That's one reason why students shouldn't be dating so young."

Is there anybody in this whole school who isn't talking about me? Sophie thought on the way to the cafeteria. It felt like she was walking down the hall naked.

When she got to the Corn Flake table in the cafeteria, the Lucky Charms were there too. Sophie didn't let her eyes linger on

Jimmy. There was still the question of whether he really thought she was mental.

Vincent, it seemed, was in the middle of clearing that up.

"That so-called quote from Jimmy was obviously taken out of context," he said.

Maggie frowned. "What does — "

"It means he said it," Fiona told her, "but not about Sophie." She didn't look all that convinced to Sophie.

"I would never say that about Sophie!" Jimmy said. She sneaked a glance. His face was blotchy.

"If you can remember when you did say it," Vincent said, "we could probably figure out who recorded you."

"We already know it was Julia and them," Maggie said. "Who else?"

"But I don't even talk to them," Jimmy said. "Except in groups in class."

"All right then." Darbie's voice was brisk. "When did you say somebody had serious mental problems?"

Jimmy frowned, then snapped his fingers. "It was when we were talking about that book we're reading. Y' know, the one where the guy stands the woman up on their wedding day and she won't let anybody touch anything, and it's like forty years later and the cake is still sitting there."

"Yeah," Willoughby said. "She *did* have some serious mental problems."

"And you said that in group," Vincent said.

Jimmy nodded.

"There you have it."

"But how did they get my screen name on there?" Sophie said. "Because I did *not* say what it says I said."

Vincent put out his hands as if that were obvious. "It's so easy for somebody to copy your screen name when you're IM'ing. They just erase what you did say and put in whatever they want."

"But she doesn't IM with the Pops," Darbie said.

"I did once," Sophie said. Her brain was finally thawing out, and things were pinging in there. "Anne-Stuart IM'd me to say she was sorry about what Julia said about me that day."

"Did you answer?" Vincent said.

"All I said was *hi* and *thanks*."

"That's all it takes." Vincent popped a whole Oreo into his mouth and added, "Like I said, there you have it."

Just then Girl #1 and Girl #2 appeared and stood at the end of the Corn Flakes' table. They looked at Sophie, looked at each other, and became hysterical. They had to help each other stay upright as they moved away howling.

"Do you believe that?" Sophie said to Fiona.

Fiona just cocked an eyebrow.

"What does that mean?" Sophie said.

"It means what I said before. It isn't just the getting-together website that's making people think this stuff about you and Jimmy."

Sophie stared at her.

"I'm just saying they see you two together all the time." Fiona shrugged. "So what else are they supposed to think?"

As much as that ate at Sophie, for the rest of the week it seemed Fiona might be at least a little bit right. It didn't matter what Sophie and Jimmy did. Whether they were working on the website in the computer room, walking to a Round Table meeting together, or practicing their scenes for the Christmas movie, there always seemed to be at least two people there, pointing and whispering and snickering behind their hands. It was never the Corn Pops or the Fruit

Loops, but Sophie constantly looked for camera lenses and tape recorders.

When she went to bed every night she tried to confess her sins, but it seemed like it was everybody else who was doing the sinning.

I know I'm supposed to forgive them, she thought more than once. *But I don't know how!* When Dr. Peter canceled Bible study at the last minute on Wednesday, she thought she might actually *develop* some serious mental problems.

Sophie was also spending every evening trying to bring her grades back up. That meant spending less and less time with the Corn Flakes, and Fiona was complaining right out in the open about that. Sophie hardly even had a chance to read and send emails, much less go to the Corn Flakes' chat room. The Subject line on Fiona's email Friday night was: *Are You Still Alive?*

You BETTER make some time for me after rehearsal tomorrow, she'd written. I'm going into Sophie withdrawal.

I'm all yours tomorrow, Sophie wrote back.

But it didn't quite turn out that way.

The whole group, even Kitty *in a wheelchair, met at the skating rink at Hampton*

9

Coliseum Saturday morning to practice the ice-skating scene for the movie. Boppa took a seat in the stands to watch.

"I don't remember any ice skating in ''Twas the Night Before Christmas,'" Maggie said for about the twentieth time.

"Whoever wrote it put it in there because you have to have action in a movie," Sophie told her patiently. She finished lacing her skates and stood up. She'd learned to skate when she was little, but it had been a while since she'd been on the ice. She put out one foot and slid into an almost split.

"That's perfect!" Vincent said. "If this scene is gonna be funny, you're gonna have to fall down a lot."

"It won't be funny if she breaks a leg," Maggie said.

Vincent blinked at her. "Are you, like, forty years old only you're disguised as a kid?"

"You ready, Sophie?" Jimmy said.

"Ready for what?" Fiona spun around on her skates and faced them both.

"The script says Mr. and Mrs. Linkhart skate together," Darbie said.

"We need to change that," Fiona said. "It won't be funny."

"Yeah, it will be," Jimmy said. "Watch this."

He grabbed both of Sophie's hands and pulled her toward him as he skated backward. She lunged forward, legs marching out stiffly behind her.

"That *is* funny!" Kitty squealed from her wheelchair.

Willoughby let out a series of poodle shrieks as Jimmy hauled Sophie all over the ice. He whipped her back and forth, held her up by the back of her sweater while her feet kicked in the air, and did a jump over her while she crouched on the ice. It was like doing gymnastics, only on skates. Sophie felt like a limp spaghetti noodle, and she could hardly catch her breath from laughing.

"It doesn't even look close to Victorian," Fiona said when Jimmy skated Sophie back over to the group.

Maggie waved the costume sketches. "You can't do all that in a corset."

"Bummer," Nathan said. "I liked it."

"I say we cut the ice-skating scene," Fiona said.

Sophie stared at her, but Fiona wouldn't meet her gaze.

"We can do the funny stuff *and* be Victorian," Jimmy said. "We'll just go along all serious and proper, and then Sophie'll fall and I'll catch her. We'll do one of those moves we were just doing, and then we'll go back to proper."

"But we haven't seen you do anything 'proper,'" Darbie said.

"Sophie can't skate that good," Maggie said.

Sophie squirmed. *Is it just me*, she thought, *or are my best friends not being very nice to me right now?*

She looked at Willoughby and Kitty, who were watching Fiona like they were waiting for a cue. Neither of them said anything.

"Let's see what you got," Vincent said.

Fiona rolled her eyes, but Jimmy grabbed Sophie's hand again and pulled her back out into the rink.

"Just relax and do whatever I tell you," he murmured. "I won't let you fall."

Sophie gave one more glance to the doubtful group on the sidelines. Even Boppa was leaning forward in his chair.

"Okay," she whispered back.

Jimmy put one arm around Sophie's waist and stretched the other one across the front of him to hold her right hand. "Just put your left hand on my back," he whispered.

She did.

"Now relax and let me do all the work," he said.

Relax? How could she do that when she knew she was turning red all the way to her toes. Getting slung around was one thing, but this was more like dancing.

With a boy.

I don't want to do this! she thought.

She glanced toward the sidelines. Fiona was already shaking her head, an I-told-you-so scrawled across her face. Kitty appeared to be biting her nails.

"Ready?" Jimmy whispered.

Louisa Linkhart looked into her husband's eyes. She knew how much he wanted to skate with her, even though she was terribly clumsy on the ice. What could it hurt? After all, it was

Christmas Eve — and he'd said he wouldn't let her fall. He was a superb skater —

So Louisa breathed, "Ready," and let Lincoln Linkhart guide her smoothly across the lake, his hands solid and safe, holding her up. Little by little she relaxed, and she even leaned when he leaned and laughed when he laughed. It was as if they were one person, sailing past the other skaters under the moonlight. It was magic —

"Okay," Jimmy said, "when we go into the next turn, I'm gonna let go. You pretend you're falling and go all spastic. I promise I'll catch you."

"It won't take much pretending!" Sophie said — and then suddenly she was free on the ice. She flung out her arms and churned her legs to keep her balance. Laughter erupted from the sidelines.

Just as she was sure Jimmy was going to back out on his promise, he swung her back into place, and they were skating like a mature Victorian couple again. It was so real, Sophie could almost feel the corset around her middle.

"Smile when we pass them," Jimmy said.

They both turned their heads and grinned as they floated past the Charms and Flakes. Boppa was standing up, clapping, and Darbie was filming, and the others were all smiling and waving.

All except Fiona.

When Jimmy and Sophie skated up to them, it was hard to sort out which "That was perfect!" and "You guys rock!" was coming from whom. While that was going on, Fiona pulled Sophie over to the bench. Her face was as stern as Miss Odetta's.

"I know you don't want to make a fool of yourself, Soph," she said as she untied Sophie's skates. "And I'm telling you this because I'm your best friend. That really isn't going to work for the movie."

Sophie slid her foot out of Fiona's reach. "Everybody said it was good."

"They just don't want to hurt your feelings."

You're doing enough of it for everybody, Sophie wanted to say. She bit her lip.

"And besides," Fiona said, "what about when your parents see the movie?"

"What about it?" Sophie said.

"Hello! You're all snuggled up to Jimmy, holding hands. He had his arm around you, for Pete's sake!"

"That's the way they skated back then!"

"Yeah, but this isn't back then." Fiona gave Sophie her I-know-more-than-you-do-about-this look. "Listen to me, for once. Aren't you having enough trouble with everybody accusing you of being practically engaged to the guy? Think what they'll do with this."

"Nobody at school's going to see our movie for church," Sophie said.

Fiona swept an arm in the air. "Look around. There are kids from Poquoson all over the place here. You and Jimmy looking like you're attached at the hip is Internet material, Soph."

For an instant, Sophie started to go cold. And then something pinged in her mind.

"You know what, Fiona?" Sophie said. "I'm going to keep the power to be myself. Jimmy and I were working on the movie out there. It was embarrassing, but I was *trying* to play my part."

Fiona knotted her lips. "Other people don't know that."

"'Other people' can think what they want."

"And they will," Fiona said.

"Then let them."

Sophie looked at her until Fiona stood up. "Then don't come whining to me when it's all over that *getting together* website," Fiona said. She started back toward the group.

"Are you sleeping over at my house tonight?" Sophie said.

Fiona didn't look back. "I can't," she said.

Suddenly, Sophie was very cold.

Fiona sat in the front with Boppa on the way home and didn't say much to anyone. She barely said good-bye to Sophie when Boppa dropped her off. Everybody else looked like they would rather be having their teeth cleaned.

What just happened? Sophie thought as she trudged up the stairs to her room.

She was lying on her bed, trying to find an answer in the curtains above her head, when Lacie poked her head in.

"Good, you're not online," she said.

Sophie blinked and smiled vaguely.

Lacie squinted at her and crawled onto the bed. "Okay, what's going on? Tell me those little Popettes weren't at the skating rink."

Sophie shook her head. "They're everywhere else. They even have Fiona believing that I'm going out with Jimmy—and I'm *not!*" Sophie raked her fingers through her hair. "Sometimes I don't care what people think—but then I do!"

"Is it that website you were telling Daddy about?"

"That's part of it." She told Lacie about Fiona, and about the picture that had appeared on everybody's camera phones.

"Can you prove it was the Pops?" Lacie said.

"No. They're being really careful. I know I'm supposed to ignore it, but it's hard! I'm used to telling them to their faces that they're not getting to me."

Lacie rolled over onto her stomach and propped her chin in her hand. "This time they *are* getting to you. You know why, don't you?"

"Do you?"

Lacie put on her Wise Big Sister face. "Because you can't get away from it. You turn on your computer in your own house and there they are. And if you stay off the computer, you're out of the loop."

Sophie nodded for her to go on.

"Besides that, you can't really go up to them and say, 'Back off,' because you aren't absolutely sure it's them. And by now, so many people are involved, they're probably taking it and doing their own thing with it."

"This isn't making me feel better," Sophie said. "I don't even want to go back to school now. Maybe Kitty's mom can home-school me with her."

Lacie rolled her eyes. "First of all, that isn't going to happen. And second of all, you still can't let them have control over you. Next thing you know, you'll be escaping into Dream Land again and messing up in school."

Sophie gulped.

"You already have," Lacie said.

"I have *two* characters I can run to now," Sophie said.

Lacie sat up. "Okay, Miss Multiple Personality Disorder, you can't let this happen. If it's affecting your grades and your best friendships, you have to stop it."

"I don't know how!"

"Hel-*lo*! You just put together a whole website on it. You don't have any evidence that could point to those little vixens?"

"No."

"Who told you about the Getting Together website in the first place?"

Sophie thought hard. "I don't know. I got an email from some-body I didn't know, and like a stupid head I opened it. It told me to check out the getting together thing."

"Did you delete it?"

"I don't think so."

Lacie headed for the door. "Then it's still in your old mail. Let's get it off and give it to Daddy. He can find out who sent it."

"What do I do about Fiona and the Flakes?" Sophie said as she followed Lacie downstairs.

"Whatever you do," Lacie said, "do it face-to-face."

They printed out the mystery email for Daddy, and he asked Sophie to forward it to his email. Then he told her he was going to buy some software that would allow him to monitor what went in and out of Sophie's computer.

"Dad-dy!" she said.

"It's not that I don't trust *you*, Baby Girl. It's these other kids that are running wild all over the Internet." He put his hand under her chin and tilted her head up. "Meanwhile, you stay strong. Don't let the other team intimidate you."

But Sophie didn't feel right then like she even had a team of her own. And there seemed to be only one thing she could do about that.

The next morning at church, she gathered the girls in the hall before Sunday school started.

"I want to know if you all believe me when I say I don't like Jimmy as a boyfriend," she said. "Tell me to my face."

Everybody looked at Fiona.

"What about it?" Sophie said to her. Her stomach was squirming.

"If he isn't your boyfriend," Fiona said, "then why do you spend more time with him than you do with me — us?"

"You spent four hours with just him last week," Maggie said, "and none with just us."

"You were keeping track?" Sophie said.

"I hardly even got an email from you," Kitty said.

"We're not trying to make you feel guilty, Sophie," Darbie said. "But you asked."

Willoughby tucked her arm through Sophie's. "We know he's cute and everything—"

"Would you stop?" Sophie pulled herself away. "What do I have to do to prove to you that—"

"Spend more time with us," Fiona said. "And less time with Jimmy." Her eyes narrowed. "That Round Table website has to be planned by now."

"It is," Sophie said. "Mrs. Britt's got it."

"Then you could be with us before school," Fiona said.

"Well, yeah," Sophie said.

"I told you she'd do it!" Willoughby all but did a backflip.

"Uh-oh," said a familiar voice down the hall. "I see trouble."

It was Dr. Peter, grinning and wearing a sling on his arm.

Sophie's heart turned over.

"What happened?" they all said in unison.

"I had a little fender bender Wednesday afternoon," Dr. Peter said. "That's why I had to cancel Bible study. But I'll be back this week."

"Does it hurt?" Maggie said.

Dr. Peter sucked in air. "Yeah, but I'm man enough to handle it. So what's going on here?"

"Sophie's just getting her priorities straight," Fiona said.

While Fiona launched into a definition of *priorities* for Maggie, Sophie closed her eyes.

I think that means I figured out what's important, she thought.

But she wasn't so sure that was what had just happened.

And she was even less sure later that day.

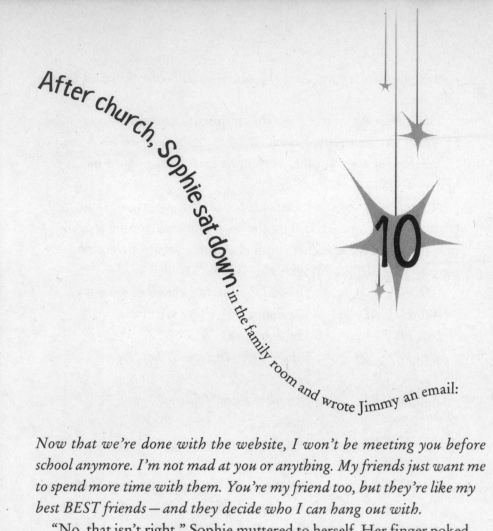

After church, Sophie sat down in the family room and wrote Jimmy an email:

Now that we're done with the website, I won't be meeting you before school anymore. I'm not mad at you or anything. My friends just want me to spend more time with them. You're my friend too, but they're like my best BEST friends — and they decide who I can hang out with.

"No, that isn't right," Sophie muttered to herself. Her finger poked at the delete key. A message popped up on the screen:

Your Mail Has Been Sent

"No!" Sophie cried. "Not *send!* Delete!"

But there was no getting it back — and suddenly she wanted that more than anything. She confessed to

Jesus right on the spot. And she added to it, *Please don't let Jimmy hate me.*

Then she sat staring at the monitor, shoulders sagging. Maybe if she let the Flakes know what she'd done to keep their friendship, she would feel better. At least they would believe her now.

Nobody seemed to be available for instant messaging, and an email meant waiting too long for an answer, so Sophie logged into the Corn Flakes' chat room. The screen names were popping up like snapping fingers.

CHEER:	*She said she would be with us more now.*
WORDGRL:	*She didn't WANT to say it.*
IRISH:	*She didnt promise.*
MEOW:	*Sophie keeps her word!!!!!! She luvs us!!!!!!*
WORDGRL:	*I think she luvs J more.*
CHEER:	*no way.*
WORDGRL:	*You saw them skating.*
IRISH:	*She was acting.*
WORDGRL:	*Not when we were talking after. She's way serious about him.*
MEOW:	*She's lying???!!!!*
IRISH:	*Maybe she doesn't know she's lying.*
CHEER:	*huh?*
WORDGRL:	*She doesn't know WHAT she's doing. We have to set her straight.*
DREAMGRL:	*Don't bother. I think I have it pretty straight already.*

With tears in her eyes, Sophie logged off before any of her friends could respond.

Her former friends.

She didn't go near the Internet for the rest of the evening. In fact, she didn't go into the family room at all after supper. The computer was suddenly a cyber-monster, waiting to devour her.

But her room, her haven, was a lonely cave, and so was she. It was as if everything had been hollowed out and she was just a Sophie-shell. She groped around for an exit.

Cynthia Cyber was more determined than ever to clean up the Internet. When friends turned against friends, the Web was no longer a healthy place to be. If only Dot Com and the others had not gossiped about her in the chat room as if she were some silly, boy-crazy—

"But they did!" Sophie said out loud. Especially Fiona. *She said I was lying. How could she THINK that?*

Louisa Linkhart smoothed her hands over her corseted waist and went to the library door, her gown swishing as she hesitated in the doorway. Lincoln was there, his head bent over the paper he was writing on. She hated to disturb her husband, but she so needed his advice about her friends. He was so wise and so good. It would only take a moment—

She tapped lightly on the door frame and waited for him to look up, waited for his straight-teeth smile. But there was no smile as he turned to her. There was only hurt in his very-blue eyes—

Sophie leaned against her closet door and scrunched her eyes closed. *I wish I could talk to Dr. Peter right now*, she thought. *I will on Wednesday.*

Right. At Bible study. Where all the girls she thought were her friends would be waiting to "straighten her out."

Sophie crawled onto her bed and let the tears come.

Monday was the hardest day ever. It was the last week before Christmas vacation, but Sophie couldn't join in the gift-exchanging and the classroom-door decorating. She was too busy making herself invisible so she could avoid the Corn Flakes.

She hung out in Miss Imes' room before school, because she knew the Flakes would never guess she'd be anywhere close to math if she didn't have to be. Even when Miss Imes told her that as a Christmas present she was dropping everyone's lowest grade, it didn't help.

Sophie bolted out of first-second block when the bell rang and changed into her PE clothes in a bathroom stall. When she saw there was no getting away from the Flakes in the roll-check line, she told Coach Yates she had a stomachache and needed to go to the nurse. It was the truth. She had never felt sicker.

When she walked through the gym toward the locker room to change her clothes at the end of the period, Eddie Wornom was putting away the tumbling mats. Sophie pretended not to see him, but that became impossible when he said, "Hey. Sophie."

This is NOT the time to start showing your real self, Sophie thought. She said, "Hey," and kept walking. Eddie caught up with her.

"I know how you feel," he said.

That stopped Sophie with a squeal of her tennis shoes. *There is no way YOU know how I feel, Eddie Wornom,* she wanted to say. Instead, she just looked up at him and waited.

"I'm not hanging out with my old friends, either," he said.

And you're telling me this because—

"They do stuff I can't do anymore," Eddie went on. "So now they're doin' that stuff to *me.*"

"They're bullying you?" Sophie said.

She almost added, *Serves you right.* But Eddie's eyes were drooping at the corners. She had seen other eyes look that same way, that very morning in her own mirror.

"Got those mats up, Mr. Wornom?" Coach Virile called from the doorway.

"I gotta go," Eddie said to Sophie. "If you need any help — "

He shrugged again and went back to the mats. Sophie broke into a run for the door, but Coach Virile didn't move.

"Big change in our man Eddie, huh?" he said.

Sophie swished her foot back and forth in front of her and watched it.

"I'll take that as an I-don't-think-so," Coach said. He waited until Sophie looked up at him. "Miracles do happen, Little Bit. You might want to hear what he has to say."

It occurred to Sophie as she hurried to the locker room that there was certainly no *other* kid she could talk to right now. But Eddie Wornom?

Lunch was the biggest challenge. Sophie escaped to the courtyard, but she didn't feel like eating. Toward the end of lunch, she heard an announcement over the intercom that the new Round Table website was now up and running, and everyone who planned to use a school computer from then on had to sign the AUP. Even that didn't lift her up.

When she got to Mr. Stires' class, there was a note on her desk, folded like a bird the way only Fiona did it.

She could feel Fiona watching her. If I read it I'll start crying, Sophie told herself. And they'll know how much I miss them already.

Sophie swallowed hard. She was probably going to cry even without reading it.

It wasn't hard to get a restroom pass out of Mr. Stires, although he did crinkle his mustache a little as he said, "Are you okay, Sophie?"

All she could do was nod, and in the restroom she slammed her way into a stall and sobbed. Only when she started to calm down did she realize she still had Fiona's note clutched in her hand. She fumbled it open.

We didn't do anything wrong, it said. We're just trying to help you. Du-uh — we're your best FRIENDS!

Friends don't call you a liar! Sophie wanted to shout. Without reading the rest, she crumpled the note and pitched it into the trash can.

In sixth period there was no getting away from them because they all had seats together, the Flakes and the Charms. Sophie stood in the doorway, debating whether to ask for another pass to the nurse or just crawl under her desk, when Nathan was suddenly beside her. His face looked like the inside of a watermelon, minus the seeds.

"They want to know if you're rehearsing after school," he said. He spoke so low Sophie had to move her ear closer to his mouth.

"Excuse me," B.J. said behind them. "Other people need to get in."

Sophie moved, but B.J. still grazed her, knocking Sophie against Nathan. Sophie had to stay there until the rest of the Corn Pops strolled into the room. Julia flung a look over her shoulder at her.

"Can't make up your mind which boy you want, Soapy?"

Sophie looked frantically at Nathan, whose scalp had gone scarlet between his curls.

"So, are you gonna come?" Nathan managed to get out.

Julia and Anne-Stuart waited, as if he'd asked *them* the question.

"Yeah," Sophie said. "I'll be there."

Nathan skittered to his desk, but Julia didn't move. When Sophie tried to get around her, she said, "So, does this mean Jimmy is available again?"

All Sophie could do was stare at her.

"I'll take that as a 'yes,'" Julia said. She started to walk away, and then she stopped. "Oh, and by the way — that AUP thing we're supposed to sign? Nobody's going to follow that." With a victorious toss of her hair, she was gone.

"You still sick, LaCroix?" Coach Yates said. "You're looking a little green."

"Yes, ma'am," Sophie said. "Could I go to the nurse again?"

She spent all of sixth period lying on a cot, trying not to imagine what rehearsal was going to be like. She had been careful not to even look at Jimmy all day, and he hadn't talked to her, either. He'd even sent Nathan to ask her if she was coming.

How am I going to pretend I'm his wife? she thought.

Louisa Linkhart wiped the last of the tears from her eyes with her lace handkerchief. She had to do what a good Victorian wife did. She must go to Lincoln and beg his forgiveness, even if she had to get down on her knees — which was no easy feat in a corset and petticoats —

Sophie sat straight up on the cot. Of *course*! She could almost imagine Dr. Peter right there, saying, *Du-uh, Loodle. Didn't we talk about forgiveness? Weren't you listening?*

The tears came again and there wasn't a lace handkerchief in sight. The nurse peeked in and then opened the door wide.

"Honey, do you want me to call your mom to come get you?" she said.

"No," Sophie said. "There's something I have to do after school."

As soon as the bell rang, Sophie dodged through the crowd in the hall to Jimmy's locker. To her relief he was there, but so were Nathan and Vincent. When he saw Sophie, Vincent poked Jimmy in the back and pointed. The very-blue eyes that looked at her came straight out of her daydream.

"I need to talk to Jimmy." Sophie's voice squeaked, but she didn't care. She had to get this out.

"Oh, so now you want to talk to him," Vincent said. His own voice matched hers, squeak for squeak.

"It's okay," Jimmy said. "I'll catch up with you guys."

Nathan tore out of there like he was being chased by a pack of dogs. Vincent shrugged as he passed. "I don't get girls," he said.

Jimmy stuffed some books into his locker, and then pulled the same ones out. Sophie was feeling smaller by the second, but she straightened her shoulders. This would be so much easier if she were wearing a corset.

"I was stupid," she blurted out. "Fiona and them were all complaining because I was spending all that time working on the website with you and I felt guilty and I didn't want to mess things up with them — only I like being friends with you but I didn't know what to do especially with all the stupid rumors and that website about us — I thought I needed my friends to help me — only I should have told them I could be friends with you *and* them and that's what I was going to do but I hit Send instead of Delete and I think I hate the Internet now — "

"Sophie," Jimmy said.

"What?" Sophie said.

"Take a breath."

Sophie took a huge one. "Will you forgive me? Because I'm *really* sorry."

"Sure," Jimmy said.

Sophie blinked. "That's it? You're just going to forgive me just like that?"

"Yeah. Why not?"

"Then — we're still friends?" Sophie said.

"We're cool," Jimmy said. "Only — "

Sophie held her breath again. Here it came.

"I'm not the one you gotta worry about," he said. "Fiona and the girls, they don't get why you're not speaking to them."

"They don't *get* it? They said I was a liar!"

"About what?"

"About — nothing." Sophie drove her fingers through her hair. "I don't think they're even sorry for what they wrote about me."

"Whatever it was, I don't think so," Jimmy said. "Fiona says they didn't do anything wrong." He shrugged. "I sure don't get why Fiona thinks I'm scum all of a sudden."

Sophie sank back against the lockers. "This is going to be a really weird rehearsal."

Jimmy shrugged. "We could just practice our scenes and they could do other stuff."

"You tell them that, then," Sophie said.

Sophie's stomach squirmed as she followed Jimmy to the courtyard. All of this felt so un-Corn Flake — not even being able to rehearse a film with her friends, when that was one of the main things that made them the Corn Flakes. It was heinous.

Am I making too big a deal out of this? she thought.

The aching emptiness told her no.

Am I supposed to just act like it never happened? They really hurt me, and they're not even sorry!

But maybe they were. Maybe Jimmy didn't get girls any more than Vincent did.

There was only one thing to do. Face-to-face, Lacie had told her.

When Sophie and Jimmy got to the courtyard, everybody was busy setting up. Willoughby did her poodle thing at the sight of Sophie, and then she looked at Fiona.

Fiona put down the baby Jesus doll she was carrying and put her hands on her hips.

103

"So are you going to rehearse with us?" she said.

"Can we talk first?" Sophie said.

"You mean about the fact that you've been ditching us all day?" Fiona looked at the Corn Flakes, who were all gathering nervously beside her. "We'd love to hear about that."

The little pink bow of a mouth was once again drawn into a knot. The magic gray eyes looked as hard as stones. There was no "I'm sorry" hinting around the edges of her voice.

"Never mind," Sophie said. "Let's just rehearse."

It was the worst. Everyone was so stiff and awkward, Vincent said there wasn't anything he'd caught on film that they could use. Sophie cut the rehearsal short early and ran like a bunny for the late bus. She was halfway there when a solid voice behind her said, "Sophie. Wait up."

Sophie turned to face Maggie and kept walking backward. "I can't miss the bus," she said. "My mom can't pick me up."

"Then I'll email you when I get home," Maggie said. Her face was still, like she was afraid if she moved it, it would show what was going on inside her.

"I don't think I'm ever going online again," Sophie said.

Maggie stopped. "I'm still gonna email you."

Sophie could only nod as she turned away. There was too much confusion in her head for anything to break free and make sense.

None of it got sorted out on the way home, not even when she tried to be Louisa Linkhart or Cynthia Cyber. Even imagining Jesus didn't give her any answers. When she got home, Mama was sound asleep on the couch in the family room, and there was a note saying Zeke was with Boppa. There was only Sophie and the monster computer, staring at her out of its one big monitor-eye.

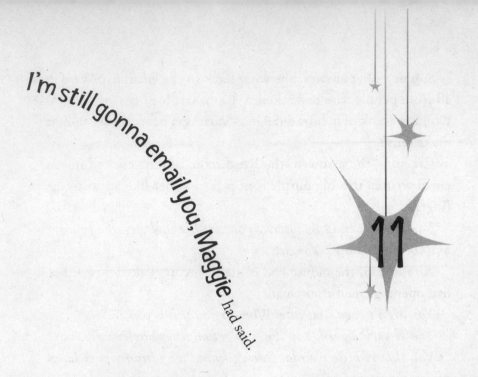

I'm still gonna email you, Maggie had said.

To tell me I'm a liar? Sophie thought. *I can't handle that!*

But the missing them, that was bigger than the being afraid. Palms sweating, she logged on with slippery fingers.

75 New Messages, the computer told her.

Seventy-five? Sophie thought. *I don't even know that many people!*

She scanned the list for familiar screen names. There were none. Maggie's email wasn't there, either. When the IM chime rang, Sophie twitched. It was from Anne-Stuart.

ANGELEYES: *Everybody's been asking me for your email address. Going out with Jimmy made you popular. How come you broke up?*

Sophie didn't answer. She went back to the email list. Were these all from people who had asked Anne-Stuart for her email address? Come to think of it, how did Anne-Stuart get her address? It didn't make sense.

Creeping the arrow to the Read icon, Sophie clicked it. An email written in a big purple font poked at her like an accusing finger.

You are a loser. Only losers go out with a cool guy like Jimmy and then dump him. You are scum.

Almost as if the mouse had come to life, it clicked down the list, opening email after email.

You aren't even that cute. Who do you think you are?

You're such a geek. You'll never get another boyfriend.

You skinny little weirdo. I don't know why Jimmy ever liked you in the first place.

Sophie didn't even realize she was sobbing until Mama's voice made its way across the room.

"Come here, Dream Girl," she said. "Don't look at that anymore. Come here."

Sophie ran to her and cried for so long with her face buried in Mama she forgot herself. Only when Lacie was suddenly there, saying, "Those hateful, evil little—freaks!" did Sophie lift her head. Her glasses were sideways on her face and salt-stained with tears, but she could see Lacie leaning over Sophie's computer, hand on the mouse.

"What are you doing?" Sophie said.

"I'm saving them and printing them out," Lacie said. "Daddy's going to want to see this."

"What is it?" Mama said.

"You don't even want to know," Lacie said.

But Mama did want to know, and when Daddy got home, they held a family conference at the coffee table.

"This has gone too far, Soph," Daddy said. "You know I have to do something."

Sophie didn't answer. It hurt too much to talk.

Daddy ran a hand over his head. "'Course, there may not be anything the school can do if none of this came from school computers. Not unless the effects of it have spilled over into school." He put a big hand on Sophie's shoulder. "Now tell me the truth, has this harassment started to affect your grades?"

"Yes," Sophie said. Her voice sounded like wood.

Mama stirred on the couch. "The school nurse called and said she saw you twice today, Dream Girl."

"This stuff would make me sick too," Lacie said. She scowled at the handful of emails she was holding. Her eyebrows puckered at the top one. "I know this address. Katie Schneider uses this one — does she have a sister or brother at the middle school?"

"There's B.J. Schneider," Sophie managed to say. "She's one of the Corn Pops."

"Hello!" Lacie said.

"It's a start anyway." Daddy smothered Sophie's shoulder with his hand again. "I'll see Mr. Bentley first thing in the morning. For right now, I want you to stay off the Internet completely."

"That's so not fair," Lacie said. "She's the victim and she gets the punishment."

"I'm not punishing, I'm protecting," Daddy said. "It's the same reason I had to cut down Zeke's giant yarn Spider-Man web — so he wouldn't get hurt." He let go of Sophie's shoulder. "I'm just shielding you from a different kind of web, Baby Girl."

That's me, all right, Sophie thought. *Baby Girl.*

But she nodded at Daddy. There was nobody to email anyway.

"Hey, look," Lacie said. "It's snowing!"

Suddenly it was all about the snow, which almost never happened in Poquoson. It put Mama in a Christmas mood, and within five minutes she had Lacie baking cookies and Sophie bringing her pen and paper to make lists.

"I'm going to direct Christmas right from this couch," Mama said. She patted her tummy. "You and me, little girlfriend."

Sophie didn't feel at all like Christmas. All she felt was sadness for her baby-sister-to-be. She was coming into a world where you couldn't even turn to your best friends when everybody else was ripping you apart.

There was no school the next day because of the snow. Although Mama tried to keep everybody focused on holiday preparations, Sophie spent most of her time upstairs wrapped in a blanket because she was cold from the inside out. She couldn't even stand to be in the same room with her computer.

When more snow came Tuesday night and the TV announced Wednesday morning that the roads were so bad school would be closed again, Sophie wasn't sure whether to cheer or cry. She decided it didn't matter. She was still going to feel like someone had kicked out her soul no matter where she was.

A little before lunchtime, Dr. Peter called.

"No Bible study class today, Loodle," he said. "Du-uh, huh?"

"That's okay," Sophie told him. "I wasn't going to come anyway."

"Oh?"

"I can't be around the Corn Flakes. I don't think we're friends any-more."

"Impossible!" Dr. Peter said.

"That's what *I* thought," Sophie said, and then she burst into tears.

"Are you up for a visitor?" he said in a husky-soft voice. "Let me talk to your mama."

Dr. Peter was there within half an hour, and Lacie set them up in Daddy's study so they could have privacy — since Zeke was home too.

Sophie wrapped up in the blanket she'd dragged from upstairs and curled up in Daddy's desk chair. But before he sat down, Dr. Peter said, "I realized on the way over here that I didn't even ask you if you wanted to talk to me about this."

"I do!" Sophie said. "I'm all tangled up in knots like I used to get, only Cynthia Cyber and Louisa Linkhart can't even help me. I have *two* dream characters, and I'm still confused." She took a breath. "And I *have* been talking to Jesus."

"I have no doubt."

"I've confessed every sin I ever committed."

Dr. Peter's eyes twinkled, but he didn't smile. At least *he* took her seriously.

"Then it's a sure thing you're forgiven, Loodle," he said. "Why don't you start from the top?"

Sophie told him everything, which took a while since there were so many parts to it. Her voice got higher and higher as she talked, so that by the time she got to the heinous emails, she could hardly hear herself. She pulled the blanket tighter, but she still felt like an ice cube.

Dr. Peter crossed one foot over the other knee and wiggled it. "This is huge for you, Loodle," he said. "I think we need to unpack it, like a suitcase. You want to start with the Corn Flakes?"

Sophie's stomach squirmed, but she nodded.

"The problem is, how are you going to be able to forgive them, right?" Dr. Peter said.

"How *can* I forgive them?"

"Like I said, God has forgiven you. Jimmy forgave you too, right?"

"But I told him I was sorry," Sophie said. "Fiona and the other girls, they don't even think they did anything wrong." She pulled at her hair. "Am I supposed to just pretend it didn't happen?"

Dr. Peter waggled his head back and forth. "Yes and no."

"How can it be both?"

"Okay, let's keep it simple. We have to try to handle forgiveness the way God does. We'll never get it totally right," he added as Sophie opened her mouth to protest. "But we have a responsibility to try."

"I'll never even get close," Sophie said. "But what do I have to lose?"

"That's my Loodle. Okay, think about the story we read last time. The master represented God, right?"

"Yes."

"And he forgave the servant. So there's your first step."

"But — "

"Even though it meant he wouldn't get paid back, the master let it go."

Sophie sat up and thought about that. "So, even if I don't get to hear them say they were wrong, I have to let it go."

"That's where the yes and the no come in." Dr. Peter rubbed his hands together. "Yes, the master forgave him, and the servant got off easy — but it didn't change him. So the next time the servant messed up, it was off to jail. When you forgive somebody, that doesn't mean she gets to escape her responsibilities."

"So — yes, I forgive the Corn Flakes. But — no, I don't just let them get away with hurting me." Sophie flopped back in the chair. "But I don't get how!"

"The whole reason for forgiveness isn't so people can just keep on doing stupid things," Dr. Peter said. "It's so people can have another chance to get it right."

Sophie considered that. "You mean, like a teacher dropping your lowest grade."

"Sure. And when somebody really feels like they've been forgiven, sometimes that changes something in them and they're better people." Dr. Peter wiggled his eyebrows. "Other times, you, the forgiver, have to help them."

Sophie looked down at her lap. "I want to forgive them — but it hurts so much."

"God never said it was going to be painless. But when you don't do it — well, what happened to the servant when he didn't forgive the guy who owed *him*?"

"He got thrown in jail for, like, six years."

"How did it feel when Jimmy forgave you?"

"Good!"

"And when a teacher drops that grade — "

"Relieved."

"And how about all the confessing you've been doing — does it help?"

"I think so."

Dr. Peter sat back, arms folded. "We'll only know that if you can find it in yourself to forgive your Corn Flakes."

Sophie felt the ping in her head. "So I forgive them, because that's what God does, and if they really get it they won't do that again, but I might have to help them."

Dr. Peter held up his palm. "That's it, Loodle," he said as Sophie high-fived him. "I think you can take it from here. You want to pray with me?"

After they talked to God together and Dr. Peter left, Sophie still wasn't completely sure what she was going to say. But she took the phone into her room. Her hand shook as she punched in Fiona's number.

"It's me," Sophie said when Fiona answered. Then, before she could chicken out, she plunged on. "I forgive you for not believing me about Jimmy — and for talking about me in the chat room. Even if you don't think you did anything wrong, I'm still gonna forgive you and I still want to be your friend because you're a good person and you'll figure it out and if you don't, I'll help you."

There was silence. Sophie's heart sagged.

Finally, Fiona said, "I'll send you an email."

"I can't —," Sophie started to say.

But the phone clicked in her ear. After that, she didn't even try to call the other girls. She just sat on her bed with the phone in her lap and closed her eyes.

I tried, Jesus, I really tried, she prayed. *It didn't work out the way it was supposed to.*

From the look in his kind eyes, she was pretty sure he knew exactly how she felt. He'd probably been there himself.

Sophie and Daddy got to GMMS early the next morning so Daddy could talk to Mr. Bentley. He had the emails in his briefcase.

"I can't make any promises, Soph," he said before they got out of the truck. "But I'll sure go to bat for you."

I don't think it's gonna do any good, Sophie thought. *It's probably going to make things worse.*

Daddy put his hand on her shoulder for about the fiftieth time since the night before. "I want you to be able to enjoy your computer the way it's meant to be used," he said. "I'm going to install some editing software on there so you and your team can do some killer stuff with your movies."

What team? Sophie thought.

"And I'm setting up a new email account for you."

"I don't think I'm ever going online again."

"You have the right to check your email without being afraid of what you're going to read. That's why I'm here."

Sophie swallowed a throat full of tears. "Thanks for trying, Daddy."

She went to her locker and was staring at her stack of books when somebody tall came up beside her. It was Eddie Wornom.

"Hey," he said.

It wasn't an I'm-about-to-make-your-life-a-walking-nightmare 'hey,' so she said "Hey" back. Besides, Coach Virile had told her to give it a chance.

"Coach Nanini says we have a lot in common," he said.

"Coach Nanini says *we* have something in common?" She didn't add, *Is he mental?*

"He said I should keep trying to talk to you, 'cause I've been getting cyber-bullied too."

Sophie let her locker slam shut and stared at him.

"I know," Eddie said. "It used to be, I woulda been the one doing it. That's probably why they're doing it to me now, because like I told you, I won't do that stuff anymore."

Half of Sophie wanted to say, *Do you think I'm a TOTAL moron?* But the other half saw his eyes drooping again.

"Okay," she said with a heavy sigh. "We can talk—only not here."

"Coach Nanini said we could talk in the gym."

Why am I doing this? Sophie asked herself as they walked in silence to the gymnasium. *Don't I have enough problems?*

She was about to change her mind and bolt when Eddie held the gym door open for her. Since he didn't trip her on the way in, she sighed and sat down with him on the lowest row of bleachers.

"I didn't go to military school," he said. "My mom sent me to this boot camp run by a bunch of Christians. Nobody believes it, but it totally changed me."

Sophie squinted at him. "You do look different."

"I *am* different. I'm not a bully anymore, only the people I thought were my friends say I'm a loser now, and the people that always hated me look at me like, 'He's fakin' it. He's gonna do somethin' any minute.'"

"Yeah," Sophie said, "that's what we were thinking."

As soon as she said it, she was sorry. But Eddie just nodded.

"Coach said it was gonna take people a while to trust me. What am I supposed to do 'til then, though?" Eddie cracked a knuckle. "I almost helped Tod and them with some stuff, just so they wouldn't ditch me. I didn't, but it stinks being by yourself all the time."

"Tell me about it," Sophie said.

"It wouldn't be that bad if they would just leave me alone, but no — they gotta attack me on websites." His fists doubled in his lap. "It makes me wanna punch somebody — and I can't go there. I'm outta chances."

"They have a website about you?" Sophie said.

Eddie uncurled his hands and picked at a cuticle. "It's not just about me — it's about everybody they hate at GMMS." He looked at her sideways. "You're on there too."

Sophie covered her mouth with both hands. She was that sure she was going to throw up.

"Don't go to it," Eddie said. "I'm not even gonna tell you what it says. I just thought — maybe — " He sprawled back against the bleachers. "Coach says we could probably help each other get through this. I don't know. If I bust those guys, I might as well just change schools."

The bell rang, and Coach Nanini appeared in the doorway. "You two need a couple of passes to class?"

Eddie didn't say anything else until Coach handed him a pass. Then he said to Sophie, "You probably have more guts than I do. I could maybe help — as long as you don't use my name."

Sophie squinted through her glasses as she watched him lope across the gym. *He's kind of being a coward*, she thought. *But, then, who could blame him?*

"You know," Coach Virile said as he scratched his signature on her pass, "the people who get forgiven for the most stuff usually change the most, Little Bit." Then he shook his head. "You might be just a smidgeon of a person on the outside, but you have a mighty spirit."

Feeling less than mighty, Sophie left the gym.

12

"You're wanted in Mr. Bentley's office, Sophie."

"Busted," Colton said.

Before Sophie even got to the door, she saw Julia pass her phone to Colton.

I'm about to be a text message, she thought. She didn't see why Lacie even wanted a cell phone. Sophie didn't want any of it — ever.

Daddy was still there when she reached Mr. Bentley's office. They were sitting in chairs in front of the principal's desk, looking like old buddies.

"I'm impressed with your father, Sophie," Mr. Bentley said as Sophie sat down facing them. He rubbed his salt-

and-pepper beard. "Most parents aren't paying attention to what's going on on the Internet."

Daddy smiled at her. "Sophie's taught me a lot about standing up for what's right."

Sophie stopped clutching the arms of her chair. Mr. Bentley shifted in his.

"I've told your dad," he said, "that I'll try to help, but unfortunately if nothing that's happened outside the school can be linked to anything here, my hands are tied. However, I am going to contact some parents, particularly Anne-Stuart Riggins' mother and B.J. Schneider's." Mr. Bentley held up two computer printouts. "They both sent you emails from their moms' email accounts at work. That's why you didn't recognize them." He rubbed his beard again. "We have all the parents' email addresses in case of emergency."

"It's a start," Daddy said.

Sophie tried not to picture Anne-Stuart coming after her, sniffing and snorting like a bull, with B.J. and the rest of her mob behind her.

"Now," Mr. Bentley went on, "as for Anne-Stuart copying your screen name from an instant message, that's very likely. However, we can't prove it."

Sophie nodded. She pretty much already knew that.

Daddy leaned forward in his chair, toward Sophie. "But," he said, "there are some things we *can* prove."

"You can?" Sophie said. "What?"

"I'll tell you later." Daddy looked at Mr. Bentley. "I *will* get that website taken down. I'm willing to take legal action, although I hope it doesn't come to that."

Legal action? Sophie thought. She squirmed in the seat—until Daddy looked at her in a way he never had before. Almost like she was another grown-up.

"She's mature for her age," he said, "but I still have to do what I can to protect her."

Sophie heard a ping in her head. It seemed to say, right out loud, *Aren't you glad he's in your loop?*

"I admire that." Mr. Bentley leaned toward Sophie too. "But I do want to remind you that none of what's been said about you is true. Try not to let it get to you."

Daddy tilted his head. "Don't you remember being twelve years old, Mr. Bentley?" He looked at Sophie. "It's the most vulnerable time in your life. Words stab you, whether they're true or not."

Sophie smiled at him. It was *her* turn to be impressed with her father.

Daddy gave her a hug before she left Mrs. Bentley's office, and that made her feel safer than she had in days — until she reached the waiting area. They were all there — Julia, Anne-Stuart, Cassie, B.J., Tod, and Colton. Several other kids leaned against the wall, looking terrified. The faces of the Corn Pops and Fruit Loops had nothing to do with fear.

They were tight with pure hate.

Sophie tried to erase those looks from her mind as she somehow got through the rest of first-second block. Replacing them with Jesus' kind eyes helped, but she wished she had her Corn Flakes' faces sending her courage from across the room. She couldn't even glance their way.

But when the bell rang and she hurried down the hall, they were suddenly on her — Fiona, Maggie, and Darbie. Maggie gave Fiona a shove toward Sophie.

"Fiona has something to say to you," Maggie said.

Fiona looked like she would rather throw herself down the stairs than say a word. Her magic-gray eyes were actually frightened.

"Do it," Darbie said.

"I want to," Fiona said. "But it's hard! I said it perfect in the email."

"What email?" Sophie said.

"The one I sent you — saying I'm sorry and I'm a horrible friend and I should have believed you, only I was being possessive again and I hate it when I do that — but I could hardly help it this time because it was about a boy and I don't get that yet — " Fiona took a ragged breath. "I wish you would just read the email."

"I can't," Sophie said, tears welling up. "My dad took me off the Internet because people wrote me horrible things."

"I'm glad your dad did that," Darbie said. She jammed her hair behind her ears. "Talking on the Internet is what made a bags of everything to begin with."

"I'm sorry too, Sophie," Maggie said.

"You were hardly even part of it, Mags." Fiona looked at Sophie, eyes brimming. "Mags is the one who made me be halfway brave and come to you."

"I was part of it, though," Darbie said. "I'm so, so sorry, Sophie."

Sophie could see Fiona swallowing hard. "So, do you really forgive us?" Fiona said.

Sophie watched the tears trail down Fiona's cheeks. *You never, ever cry*, Sophie thought. That was what pinged in her mind. It wasn't the words Fiona said that convinced her. It was the look in her eyes, saying, *Please, Sophie.*

You couldn't see that on a computer.

"I already told you that I forgive you," Sophie said. "All of you."

Fiona just stood there until Sophie put her arms around her and squeezed.

"We should have done this in the first place," Maggie said.

"Soph, I didn't even know I was sorry," Fiona said into Sophie's hair, "until yesterday on the phone when you told me you forgave me."

Maggie gave them both a little push. "We gotta get to PE."

"Uh-oh." Darbie nodded toward the end of the hall. Julia and Colton were heading toward them.

"They're livid," Fiona said.

The Flakes tried to hurry past them, but Colton and Julia turned and walked right along with them, one on each side, eyes blazing.

You can't see THAT on the Internet, either, Sophie thought. But she felt some of the old Sophie-courage seeping back in. They couldn't hide behind their computers this time.

"Your father and his stupid program," Julia said, pointing at Sophie.

"What program?" Sophie said.

"The one that can track emails to the senders." Colton all but spit on the floor. "What is he, the Internet police?"

Sophie lifted her chin. "Somebody has to be."

"Huh." Julia tossed her hair, catching Sophie's cheek with it. "His little program can't prove that somebody didn't hack into our email accounts — "

"And steal our screen names," Colton put in.

"Here come the rest of them," Maggie muttered.

Sophie glanced back to see B.J., Cassie, and Tod charging their way.

"Let me get this straight." Fiona stopped in front of the locker-room door. "*All* of you told Mr. Bentley somebody got into *all* your accounts and ripped off *everybody's* screen names?"

Julia looked at the group now joining them. They all nodded.

"It looks that way," Julia said.

"And not even your *daddy* can prove it didn't happen," Colton said.

"Besides." Tod pointed his whole face at Sophie. "We told them we were just messing around."

B.J. rolled her eyes. "It was just a big joke."

Darbie put her arm around Sophie. "Does it look like she's laughing?"

"It doesn't matter whether you go down for this or not," Fiona said. "We can email people and tell them it was all lies." She looked at Sophie. "Because it was."

"Whatever," Julia said.

When the Corn Pops were gone, Maggie frowned at Fiona. "I don't think we should do that email thing," she said.

"We're not," Sophie said. But she smiled at Fiona. She'd heard what she needed to hear.

Willoughby was already at the lockers when the girls got there.

"Where were you?" Sophie said.

Willoughby pulled her shirt over her head. "I'm sorry about what we said in the chat room," she said from inside it.

"I forgive everybody," Sophie said.

"Thanks." Willoughby picked up her tennis shoes and hurried out in her socks.

"What's up with her?" Fiona said.

"I know one thing," Sophie said. "I'm gonna find out. Face-to-face."

But when the Flakes got to the gym, Vincent, Nathan, and Jimmy practically knocked them down getting to them. Willoughby was with them. So was Eddie Wornom.

"What are the Fruit Loops doing with *him*?" Fiona muttered to Sophie.

Coach Yates blew her whistle. "LaCroix?" she yelled. "You kids go up in the bleachers. You have ten minutes." She glanced at Coach Virile, who was standing beside her. "Make that fifteen."

As she turned away, Coach Virile flashed ten fingers twice and grinned at Sophie.

When they were gathered on the top two rows in the corner, Jimmy nodded at Eddie. "He's got something to tell us," he said. "Coach Nanini says we can trust him."

Nobody said anything. Finally, Sophie said, "Okay, so what is it?"

Eddie blew air out of his cheeks. "I was with Tod when he stole the school email list for the whole seventh grade. He used it to tell everybody about the Getting Together website and the hate one."

"And you helped him," Fiona said. "Which is why you haven't told on him."

Eddie's forehead folded into rows as he shook his head. "I didn't help him. I just didn't tell because all of them hate me enough as it is." He blinked his eyes as if they were full of sand. "I knew if I told and they found out, Tod and Colton would wanna fight me — and it would be too hard to say no. I had to stay away from them so I wouldn't blow my last chance."

"So why tell *us*?" Vincent said. "You're the one who has to turn him in." His voice cracked like an earthquake fault.

Eddie looked at Sophie. "I want to now. But it's like, man, who's gonna back me up when they come after me?"

"I will," Sophie heard herself say.

Corn Flakes poked her from every direction. She even heard Willoughby gasp. Vincent and Nathan gave Jimmy can-you-*believe*-this-chick? looks.

But Jimmy was watching Sophie. She could almost hear the ping going off in his head.

"I'm in," he said.

Fiona sighed loudly. "Like I'm gonna let you two do it alone and get massacred. I'm in too."

Slowly the rest of the group nodded. Sophie thought Eddie might actually cry.

"Will you back me up too?" said a tiny voice.

They all looked at Willoughby, who seemed to be trying to get as small as her voice.

"Okay, *what* is going on with you?" Fiona said. "You've been acting weird all day."

Willoughby just looked at Vincent, who pulled Willoughby's cell phone out of his pocket. "I figured out how to pull up that picture of Sophie putting her pants on. Willoughby only thought she'd erased it."

Sophie had to let that sink in.

"Hello!" Vincent said. "It was taken in the locker room. This is how we link all the outside stuff to school."

Eddie gave his knuckles a crack. "That picture was on the hate website," he said.

"What hate website?" Fiona said.

Cynthia Cyber leaped from her chair at the computer desk and made a victory lap around her office. "Yes!" she shouted to Dot Com and Maga Byte and anyone else who would listen. "I've got those cyber bullies now! Their Internet harassment days are over!" She stopped and smiled broadly. "In fact, their LIVES are as much as over!"

But Louisa Linkhart smoothed the skirt of her gown and looked at her dear friends. "That is not the proper attitude," she told them. "They must be punished, yes, but their only chance for change is if we forgive them." She looked lovingly at her husband and added, "Just as we have been forgiven."

"Okay," Eddie said, "you're still the weirdest person I know." And then he shrugged and added, "But who cares?"

Coach Nanini whistled through his teeth and waved his arm.

"You ready?" Eddie said to Willoughby.

Willoughby looked at Sophie as if she were about to be dragged by the hair.

"It's okay," Sophie told her.

She was glad that Coach Nanini escorted Willoughby and Eddie, though. It was still a little hard to get used to trusting Eddie Wornom.

As the rest of them picked their way down from the bleachers, Fiona said, "If we forgive those heinous little — the Pops and the Loops — does that mean we have to hang out with them? Because I am *not* — "

"No," Sophie said. "If they change, then — "

"They're not gonna change," Maggie said.

Sophie jumped from the bottom row to the floor. "I don't know if they will," she said. "But if forgiving can change Eddie Wornom, it can change anybody."

Sophie straightened her shoulders and started toward Group Six. *Julia and Colton nudged each other, nervously*, Sophie thought. But then they stared blankly at Sophie as if they had just put on masks.

"Can't you just email them and tell them?" Fiona said as they got closer.

Sophie, Darbie, and Maggie just looked at her.

"Okay, okay," Fiona said.

Sophie had the urge to walk like she was wearing a corset. Cynthia Cyber's proof was forming accusing words in her head. But the kind eyes pushed all of that away. The kind, forgiving eyes.

Sophie and the Flakes stopped at the edge of the mat.

"Aren't you supposed to be at your own stations?" the student aide said.

Julia ignored her and stood up. "Why did Coach Nanini take Eddie and Willoughby to the office?"

"They can't prove anything," Tod said. He didn't bother to get up from the floor.

"Really?" Fiona said. "Then why are you two so nervous?"

Sophie nudged her, and Fiona sucked in her lips.

"The thing is," Sophie said to Julia and Tod, "*I* know you did it — and it was heinous — and you need to stop treating people like that. You ought to take the consequences. But — " Sophie stopped and took a deep breath. The whole gym was suddenly silent. Although Coach Yates moved in close, she didn't touch her whistle.

"But *what*?" Julia said.

"But — " Sophie breathed deeply, and with it came the old power to be who she was. "But as for me, I forgive you."

She wasn't sure she'd ever seen shock before, but she saw it now in Julia's and Tod's faces.

Any second now, they're going to laugh at me, Sophie thought.

But it didn't matter. With the Flakes and Jimmy and even Nathan behind her — and the kind eyes in her mind — she was ready.

She was ready for anything.

Glossary

appalled (a-PAWld) being really shocked, and almost disgusted, when something happens

class (klas) not a group of students, but a word that means something's really cool

embellished (em-BEL-isht) really tricky lying, like when you take the truth and add little details to make it sound better

furtively (FUR-tiv-lee) being really sneaky and not at all obvious, like an undercover spy who can't get caught

glean (gleen) to gather little bits of information to use them later

guffaw (guf-FAWW) a kind of laugh that happens when you find something really funny and can't help but laugh really loud

heinous (HEY-nus) unbelievably mean and cruel

livid (li-vid) becoming incredibly angry, and turning so red you feel like you're going to have a volcanic eruption

massacred (MAH-si-curd) to be defeated so badly that you feel absolutely destroyed

obnoxious (ub-KNOCK-shus) a person who is offensive and a complete pain in the butt, driving everyone crazy

out of context (owt of con-text) when you take something a person actually said, but make it sound completely different by repeating it in a different situation

priorities (pry-OR-uh-tees) what you think are the most important things in your life; what you give the most attention to

ravage (RA-vij) destroying something so completely that there doesn't seem to be any way to fix it

rehabilitate (re-hah-BIL-i-tate) going through a series of treatments that are meant to fix what's wrong with a person

spectacular (spek-TACK-yoo-lar) absolutely amazing, with breathtaking possibilities

vigilant (VI-jah-lent) keeping your eyes wide open and being on guard for anything bad that could happen

virile (VEER-il) the definition of manly; muscular, strong, and really hunky. Think cute movie star meets not-so-icky body builder

vulnerable (VULL-ner-uh-bull) being easily hurt or wounded; very delicate

"That is gross," Sophie LaCroix said. She turned quickly and put her

hands over her friend Willoughby Wiley's eyes. If Willoughby saw the painting, she'd probably squeal like a poodle, the way she'd been doing all morning through the entire Chrysler Museum of Art.

"I think it's *cool*," Vincent said.

Sophie cocked her head at the painting, spilling her honey-colored hair against her cheek and squinting through her glasses. "No, it isn't," she said to Vincent. "It's bloody and hideous."

"Is it totally disgusting?" Willoughby whispered.

"If you think somebody that just got their head cut off is disgusting, then, yeah," Vincent said. His voice cracked, just like it did on every other sentence he spoke.

Sophie dragged Willoughby toward the next room. Vincent shrugged his skinny shoulders and loped along beside them.

"Where's everybody else?" Willoughby said.

"They got ahead of us." Sophie looked up at Vincent as they passed through the doorway. "*They* didn't stop to look at some heinous picture of a headless person."

Fiona Bunting, Sophie's best friend, looked up from her notebook as Sophie and Willoughby headed toward her. "Oh — so you saw John the Baptist." She tucked back the wayward strand of golden-brown hair that was always falling over one gray eye and made a check mark on the page. "That one's definitely repulsive."

"Does that mean it makes you want to throw up?" Willoughby narrowed her big eyes at Vincent. "You're not gonna say we should use *that* for our project, are you?"

Sophie shook her head. "No movies about people without heads. Who would play that part, anyway?"

Willoughby grabbed her throat.

"Actually," Vincent said, Adam's apple bobbing up and down, "there are some pretty cool ways we could make it *look* on film like somebody got their head cut off — "

"No!" all three girls said together. Sophie's voice squeaked, like it did when she was really making a point.

"Okay. Chill," Vincent said.

Sophie led the way to the next painting. She was the smallest of the Corn Flakes, as she and her five friends called themselves, but they mostly followed her. It had just been that way for the sixteen months since sixth grade when they'd gotten together and decided to be the group that was always themselves and never put anybody down.

"What's this one, Fiona?" Sophie said as they stopped at the next painting.

Above them was a portrait of a sober-faced lady in a gown that looked to Sophie like it weighed three hundred pounds.

"That dress is *fabulous*!" Willoughby said with a poodle-shriek. Her hazel eyes were again the size of Frisbees.

"Aw, man," Vincent said.

"What?" Jimmy Wythe came through a door from a room Sophie hadn't gone into yet. Nathan Coffey was behind him and plowed into Jimmy's back when he stopped in front of the painting. Jimmy looked at Sophie, his swimming-pool-blue eyes begging her. "It's gonna be kinda hard to do a movie about this painting."

"She's just sitting there," Nathan said. And then his face went the color of the inside of a watermelon. Sophie expected that. Nathan always got all red when he talked, which wasn't often.

"I'm gonna go find Kitty," Willoughby said. "She is going to *love* this."

"That's what I'm afraid of," Vincent said. "I guess we could pretend she's a corpse and make the movie a murder mystery."

Fiona rolled her eyes. "She is so not dead, Vincent."

Sophie looped her arm through Fiona's. "Let's go see if Kitty and them have found anything."

"Did they?" Sophie heard Vincent ask Jimmy as she and Fiona moved into the next room.

"It's all pretty much chick stuff," Jimmy said. "I mean, not that that's all bad."

"Not if you're a chick," Vincent said.

"They are so — *boys*," Fiona said when they reached the room.

"Yeah, but at least they're not as bad as *some* boys."

That was why the Corn Flakes called Jimmy, Vincent, and Nathan the Lucky Charms — because they were way nicer than a couple of guys they referred to as the Fruit Loops. The Loops were famous for making disgusting noises with their armpits and trying to get away with launching spit missiles at people, stuff like that. Now that they'd been caught doing some really bad things, they didn't get by with as much, but they were still, to use Fiona's favorite word, heinous.

At the other end of the room, Willoughby was jabbering at light speed to the other three Corn Flakes.

"Is it a really pretty painting?" Kitty Munford said as Sophie and Fiona joined them. Her little china-doll face looked wistful. Kitty was back in school after being homeschooled while having chemotherapy for leukemia. It was as if everything were magic to Kitty in spite of her still-bald head and puffed-out cheeks.

"It's gorgeous," Willoughby said. "That dress was, like, to die for."

Darbie O'Grady hooked her reddish hair behind her ears and folded her lanky arms across her chest. "I bet the boys put the kibosh on that."

Sophie grinned. She loved it that even though Darbie had been in the U.S. for a year, she still used her Irish expressions. Between her fun way of saying things and Fiona's being a walking dictionary, the Corn Flakes practically had a language all their own. It was all about being their unique selves.

"Yeah, they hated it," Fiona said. "But we put the kibosh on John the Baptist with his head chopped off."

Kitty edged closer to Sophie until the brim on her tweed newsboy's cap brushed Sophie's cheek. "I don't want my first movie in forever to be about something gross."

"No way," Maggie LaQuita said. She shook her head until her Cuban-dark hair splashed into itself in the middle. "Kitty doesn't need that." In her stocky, no-nonsense way, she was protective of all the Corn Flakes, but especially Kitty.

"I like it that you're back with us," Sophie said to Kitty.

"This is like your first field trip in forever, huh?" Fiona said.

Willoughby raised her arms like she was going to burst into a cheer, but Maggie cut her off. Sophie was glad Maggie was the one who always enforced the rules. She would hate that job. She would have to keep her imagination totally under control to do that.

Right now, in fact, Sophie was searching for her next dream character. With a new film project to do for Art Appreciation class, she hoped one of the paintings would inspire her into a daydream that would lead to a new lead character that would shape a whole movie for Film Club to do....

"Okay — now *that's* what *I'm* talkin' about!"

Sophie looked over at Vincent, who was three paintings inside the door, bobbing his head and pointing like he'd just discovered a new vaccine. Like a flock of hens, the Corn Flakes followed Sophie to see what he'd found. Darbie and Kitty stared, mouths gaping. Willoughby out-shrieked herself.

"We can't do a movie about this," Maggie said. Her words, as always, dropped out in thuds. "Those people are naked."

Nathan turned purple.

"Painters back then were all about the human body," Fiona said. "Don't get all appalled. It's just art."

"I don't even know what *appalled* means and I think I am that." Darbie shook her head at Vincent. "You're gone in the head if you think we're going to *touch* that idea."

Sophie suddenly felt squirmy. While the three boys wandered into the next exhibit room, Sophie put her arms out to gather her Corn Flakes around her. "You guys," she said, "we're acting like the Pops and Loops, all freaking out over naked people and talking about gross things being cool."

"*We're* not doing it," Maggie said. "The *boys* are."

"They can't help it," Sophie said. "They're just boys."

Willoughby gave a mini-shriek.

"I know what you're gonna say, Soph," Fiona said. "Even if they're being a little bit heinous, that doesn't mean we have to be."

"The Corn Pops *wish* they had Jimmy and those guys in their group," Willoughby said. She looked a little startled, curls springing out from under her headband. "Sorry — Corn Flake Code — I know we're not supposed to try to make people jealous and stuff."

Fiona sniffed. "We're so beyond that."

"Don't say anything else," Darbie said out of a small hole she formed at the corner of her mouth. "Here they come."

A group of four girls made such an entrance around the corner, Sophie was sure the paintings were going to start falling off the walls. Julia Cummings sailed in the lead with her thick dark auburn hair swinging from side to side and her glossy lips set in her usual I-smell-something-funny-and-I think-it's-you curl. Fiona always said she looked disdainful.

She swept past the Corn Flakes with her three followers trailing after her, all dressed in variations of the skin-tight theme and curling their own lips as if they'd been studying Julia by the hour. There was a time when they would have stopped and made a remark about how lame and uncool each of the Corn Flakes was, but Sophie knew they didn't dare. The Corn Pops had been back in school for only a week since their last serious detention.

It was a sure thing they weren't going to take a chance with Mr. DiLoretto on their heels. He strode in right behind them, wearing his glasses with no rims and his curly grayish hair pulled back in a ponytail.

Sophie's high school sister, Lacie, had warned her about Mr. DiLoretto when the seventh graders switched from Life Skills to Art Appreciation for the new semester.

"He's a little weird," Lacie had said, "and he gets mad when people don't take art seriously."

So far, Sophie liked him fine because he let them choose their own groups for their assignment to do a creative project on any painting or sculpture they saw at this museum in Norfolk. And because he'd said their group could do a film. And because he was really nice to Kitty.

Even now he dodged the last of the Corn Pops and went straight to her.

"Have you done any sketches?" he said. His voice was always edgy, it seemed to Sophie. Like he just knew that either excitement or disaster was around the next corner.

"I did a couple," Kitty said. She giggled and opened the red sketchbook she'd been carrying around. Sophie sidled closer and felt her brown eyes bulging.

Kitty's drawings looked just like some of the paintings they'd seen on the gallery tour. The lion in one looked like it was going to leap right off the page.

"Whoa," Maggie said. "I didn't know you could draw *that* good, Kitty."

"Kathryn is an exceptional young artist," Mr. DiLoretto said.

"Who's Kathryn?" Willoughby whispered to Sophie.

Kitty giggled again. Mr. DiLoretto swept the rest of them, including the nearby Corn Pops, with a bristly look. "Expect to see incredible work from her," he said.

With another proud gaze at Kitty, he hurried on, calling over his shoulder, "You have fifteen minutes left to choose your piece, and then we gather for lunch. Cuisine and Company is on your map."

"Hey," Vincent said from a doorway. "Get a load of *this* exhibit."

As the Corn Flakes headed for him, Sophie linked her arm through Kitty's. "You're gonna be a famous artist someday," she said. "There'll be, like, an entire museum of your paintings."

"I drew a lot when I was home, you know, 'cause there wasn't that much to do." Kitty hugged the sketchbook. "Now that I'm in remission, I can do a lot more."

"Mr. DiLoretto thinks you're, like, Leonardo da Vinci or somebody," Sophie said. She could hear her voice squeaking up into mouse-range. It did that when she was delighted too.

Another voice, not delighted at all, hissed from the direction of the naked-people painting, where the Corn Pops were standing in a knot.

"Pssst!" Anne-Stuart Riggins said.

Sophie was glad they weren't closer. Anne-Stuart had a continuous sinus problem, and sometimes her sounds came out wet.

"What do they want?" Kitty muttered.

"I remember when *I* was teacher's pet," Julia said.

"We *all* were," B. J. Schneider put in.

Julia gave her a green-eyed glare and went on. "It doesn't last, though. Teachers are fickle."

"Ignore them," Sophie whispered to Kitty. She nudged her by the elbow toward the door where the rest of the group had disappeared.

"I don't know, Julia," Anne-Stuart said. She gave a juicy sniff. "If Kitty kisses up to him enough, maybe he'll keep telling her she's . . ."

She waved her hand at Cassie, who squinted her close-together eyes at the artist's name next to the nude painting and read, "Bo-ti–cel — "

"Whatever," Julia said.

"Yeah, whatever, Cassie," B.J. chimed in.

They *all* glared at B.J. this time, which gave Sophie a chance to give Kitty the final push through the doorway.

"They're always so jealous of each other," Kitty whispered. "I'm so glad I'm not a Pop anymore."

"I'm glad you're not too," Sophie said. "You never have to worry about us being all jealous and stuff."

"Sophie—look at this!"

Sophie hurried over to where the Film Club was standing, staring up at a painting of a can of Campbell's soup.

"Who would paint a stupid soup can?" Maggie said.

Fiona tapped her pen on her notebook. "Some guy named Andy Warhol."

"All his stuff is weird," Vincent said. "This one's, like, a stack of boxes."

Sophie gazed at it. "Look how real that looks."

"You thought that lady in the beautiful *dress* was boring," Willoughby said. "This would put you to sleep."

"Not movie material," Vincent said.

"If somebody was, like, *under* the boxes getting crushed," Nathan said, "that would be cool."

"That would be repulsive," Fiona said.

Sophie pulled a strand of her hair under her nose. She was glad it was long enough to do that again, because it always helped her think. Personally, she liked the funny paintings of boxes and soup cans.

"What do you think of Andy Warhol's work?"

Sophie looked up at Mr. DiLoretto.

"It's—I like it," Sophie said.

"Why?" he said.

Lacie had been right, Sophie thought. He *was* a little bit weird. She adjusted her glasses and looked back at the soup can. "Well," she said, "it's all just ordinary stuff, but up there on the wall, all shiny and perfect, it seems like it's special too."

"Well, well."

Uh-oh, Sophie thought. Did she say the wrong thing? What was it Lacie had said about him getting mad when people didn't get art?

"You have the beginnings of a good critical mind," Mr. DiLoretto said.

Sophie let go of the hair she was still pulling under her nose like a mustache. "I do?" she said.

"You don't have an ounce of talent for drawing or painting, but you show some promise as an art critic." He glanced at his watch. "Nine minutes 'til lunch . . ."

Sophie didn't hear the rest of what he said. She was gazing again at the giant soup can—

and pawing through her large canvas artsy-looking bag for her notebook and pen. Ah, there they were, beneath the camera and the portable tape recorder and her calendar full of appointments with people who wanted her expert opinion on modern art.

So many demands on my time, Artista Picassa thought. But I must make some notes on this piece because it fascinates me.

Very few people had her appreciation for the more bizarre artists like Andy Warhol. It was her duty to educate people, which was why she was an art critic. And possibly the most famous one in all of Virginia, if not beyond—

That was it, of course. Maggie could write it all down in the Treasure Book later.

They would do their project on one of Andy Warhol's pieces.

She could play Artista Picassa, the famous art critic. . . .

And maybe artists who were jealous because she didn't praise their paintings would do something heinous. . . .

Too bad they couldn't use Pops and Loops in their film. They'd be perfect as envious painters.

Sophie looked around for her group, but there was nobody left in the exhibit room.

"Rats!" Sophie said to the soup can.

She dashed into the hall, but she didn't have a clue which way to go, and the map of the museum was shoved into the bottom of her backpack.

Where's Maggie when you need her? she thought. Maggie probably had the whole layout memorized by now.

But that was why Maggie was the club's recorder and Sophie was the director. Creative people needed organized people to keep them from getting lost, Sophie decided.

The smell of food and the clattering of forks finally led her in the right direction. Mr. DiLoretto was standing in the doorway of Cuisine and Company, glaring at her from under his tangled eyebrows.

"I got caught up appreciating art," Sophie said.

He just pointed her inside. Fiona waved to her from a table across the room.

"Mr. DiLoretto wouldn't let us look for you," she said as Sophie slid into a chair.

"Tell her what we decided," Vincent said to Fiona.

"You're gonna love this, Soph," Jimmy said. His usually shy smile was wide.

Sophie looked at Fiona. "Decided about what?"

"The film," Fiona said. "Jimmy found the perfect painting for our project."

Something about the way Fiona didn't quite look back at Sophie made Sophie feel squirmy. Slipping off her shoes, Sophie pushed her toes between the close-together bars under the chair.

Maggie pushed a bowl of green soup toward her and said, "Eat."

"It looks re — what was that word?" Willoughby said.

"Repulsive," Darbie said. "It tastes better than it looks."

"It's called *The Surgeon*," Vincent said.

"The soup?" Sophie said.

"No, the painting."

"What painting?"

"The one we're going to do our project on," Fiona said.

Sophie twitched, pushing her toes farther between the tight bars, shoving them past the balls of her feet. The group had already decided? Without her?

"It's not boring at all," Willoughby said.

"And there's no blood and guts," Maggie said.

Kitty giggled. "Or naked people."

"But it's still way cool," Nathan said.

If he turned red, Sophie didn't notice. She was sure she herself was losing all color. She felt her body go rigid, and she pushed down hard again with her feet.

"I haven't even seen it," she said.

"After this, we get to go to the gift shop," Jimmy said, "and I'm gonna get a poster of it."

"All right, folks," Mr. DiLoretto said as he wove among the tables, "it's time to move on to the museum shop."

"Sophie hasn't even eaten yet," Maggie said.

"Well, now, that's her problem, isn't it?" Mr. DiLoretto said. "Kitty, you'll come with me. I want you to meet one of the artists who teaches classes here."

"Don't worry, Sophie," Darbie said, pronouncing it "Soophie" like she always did. "I've got some snacks in my bag you can eat on the bus."

Sophie didn't feel like eating. All she wanted to do was grab Fiona in the hall and find out just exactly what was going on.

But when she tried to get out of her chair, she couldn't. Her feet were stuck in the bars, and they weren't coming out.

faiThGirLz!™
Faithgirlz!™—Inner Beauty, Outward Faith

NIV Faithgirlz!™ Bible
Italian Duo-Tone™, Periwinkle
Ages 8 and up
ISBN 0-310-71012-X

Available Now

TNIV Faithgirlz!™ Bible
With TNIV text and Faithgirlz!™ sparkle! this Bible goes right to the heart of a girl's world and has a unique landscape format perfect for sharing!
Ages 8 and up

Hardcover
ISBN 0-310-71002-2

Available August 2006

Faux Fur
ISBN 0-310-71004-9

Available now at your local bookstore!

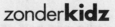

faiThGirLz!

Faithgirlz!™—Inner Beauty, Outward Faith

Now Available

No Boys Allowed:	Girlz Rock:	Chick Chat:
Devotions for Girls	**Devotions for You**	**More Devotions for Girls**
Written by Kristi Holl	Written by Kristi Holl	Written by Kristi Holl
Softcover 0-310-70718-8	Softcover 0-310-70899-0	Softcover 0-310-71143-6

Visit **faithgirlz.com**—it's the place for girls ages 8–12!!

Available now at your local bookstore!

faiThGirLz!™